Reunion at Maple Springs

A
Colin O'Brien
Maple Springs Mystery

Robert John Terreberry

Reunion at Maple Springs: A Colin O'Brien Maple Springs Mystery/
Terreberry- 1st Edition

ISBN: 978-1-7324191-7-9

1. Reunion at Maple Springs. 2. Crime Fiction. 3. Detective. 4. Noir.
5. Mystery. 6. Terreberry.

Map designed by Kathy Cherry
Cover image © 2018 Kathy Cherry

NFB Publishing

119 Dorchester Road
Buffalo, New York 14213

For more information visit
NFBPublishing.com

REUNION AT
MAPLE SPRINGS

Relax, enjoy the
reunion, you're like
family ... hope you
enjoy this lakeside
adventure.
Bob
Terreberry

Lake Erie

I-90 to Buffalo ➤

◄ I-90 to Cleveland

CHAUTAUQUA
LAKE

Mayville

Chautauqua
Belle

Route 430

Dewittville

Chautauqua
Institution

For Relief

★ Maple Springs

Route 394

Bemus Point

Slove

I-86 to Salamanca →

← I-86 to Erie

Route 430

Lakewood

Celoron

Jamestown

CHAPTER 1

Colin stood on the foot-bridge over the Maple Springs Creek looking upstream. He leaned on the metal railing and scanned the banks looking for the beaver that lived in a burrow on the creek bank somewhere just west of the Whiteside Parkway Bridge. He only saw ducks scouring the creek edges looking for tender shoots of seasonal plants that make up the usual duck diet. As he stood on the foot-bridge, the sun began setting over Lake Chautauqua behind him. He turned and saw the sun reflecting on the gush of creek water as it spilled into the lake. He had stood on this bridge many times during the past five years that he and Vonny had lived by the lake, in Maple Springs. This foot-bridge was his thinking place. All his life, wherever he lived, Colin had always found a thinking place: back porch steps, overstuffed chair in a den corner, the base of a backyard tree at his Aunt Nettie's overlooking an apple orchard. He remembered a story from his youth. It was an Uncle Remus story on a 78 RPM record of Disney's *Song of the South* movie. In the story, Br'er Rabbit was trying to escape sure death while tied to a spit over an open fire and he made up a diversionary story about a secret place, this time a laughing place. The diversion worked and the laughing place, a briar patch, distracted and ensnared his captor so Br'er Rabbit got the last laugh. Colin's secret thinking place was more strictly structured than this supposed laughing place. His thinking place had to always be in the same location, it had to be easily accessible and it always needed to give Colin a chance for rose smelling and coffee sniffing.

Today, Colin positioned himself in the middle of the bridge and looked in all directions, not finding a soul in sight. This was a major advantage to this thinking place. Colin could talk out loud to himself and could even sing with a certain volume while still not being subjected to errant listeners. Today he was practicing opening sentences to a conversation that he would surely have with Vonny within the next half hour or so. She had stayed late at work to attend a 100th birthday party for a favored resident at the nursing home where she worked, so there'd be no dinner to prepare. Colin had made himself two peanut butter and banana sandwiches, so he was all set. Vonny had recently limited her work hours to four afternoons a week so she easily extended her work day for the celebration. Colin had been retired from teaching for four years now and during each of those years, Vonny's work hours and duties lessened.

"Vonny, good news. My Uncle Ray called today. He's gonna visit The Springs, not us, but we will get to see him." There, that is all true and general, but it was sure to engender many more specific questions. Vonny always had a lot of questions.

"Hi Hon. Guess who called out of the blue today? It was Ray. He's gonna visit. Not us. He won't disturb our

summer plans. Everything we're counting on is still a go."
Sounds defensive and will surely create other obvious que-
ries.

"Uncle Ray called. He has a cottage rented in The
Springs for the summer, but he has his own agenda. We are
still on track with all of our plans." All Colin left out was
"right next door" and "starting tomorrow".

"Uncle Ray. Starting tomorrow. Right next door. All
summer. Holy crap," said Colin at level nine on a scale
of one through ten with ten being the loudest acceptable
thinking place volume.

Uncle Ray, yikes. Of all relatives to visit, it had to be
Uncle Ray. Let's see, thought Colin, he's racist, an alcohol-
ic (or at least he was), thrice married (and maybe more).
He seemed okay on the phone but then what can you tell
from a three minute telephone conversation? It could have
been Jeffrey Dahmer chatting on the other end and we all
know how he could behave. Colin hadn't seen Ray in close
to twenty years, but did get bits and pieces of information
about him from cousins, uncles and aunts. During the brief
telephone call Ray didn't say a lot. He just gave the basic
I'm-on-my-way warning. He also said they'd have to have a
heart-to-heart once he got settled.

Colin knew Vonny's first two questions and each question had to have an honest, straight forward answer. His
answers would be "next door" and "tomorrow."

After Colin said "tomorrow" out loud, he immediately

went into the lyrics of the song with that same title from the musical *Annie* that his daughter Erin had performed in years ago when she was twelve or thirteen years old.

"The Sun'll come out tomorrow.
Betchur bottom dollar that tomorrow
There'll be sun.
Just thinkin' about tomorrow
Clears away the cobwebs and the sorrow
Till there's none..."

None, thought Colin. Oh no, there'll be sorrow. Vonny never liked Ray. Never hid the fact. Perhaps it was because he was drunk at his own mother's funeral, made a real scene and left Colin with the bill, but there were surely other reasons too. Ray's mother, Katherine, Colin's grandmother was classified as a saint by all who ever knew her. She never had a harsh word for anyone and no one ever had a harsh word for her. Katherine deserved better than the disrespect of an errant son. She raised six children almost singlehandedly, including Colin's mom, Ruth. Then late in life, Raymond, who was number seven, appeared on the scene. That was how Grandma Kitty always explained Raymond's arrival; "Oh, the kids were mostly grown, two were older teens still in the house, and then Raymond Joseph appeared on the scene."

Grandma Kitty was in her late-forties and Colin's mom was twenty-two and newly married when mother and daughter had babies just three months apart. Raymond

Joseph was born first. Colin Joseph, Raymond's nephew, arrived exactly three months later. They shared a middle name that was an homage to their father/grandfather who had died earlier that same year. If truth be told, Raymie, as his mother called him, was a source of great joy to a middle-aged widow working and struggling to make ends meet and trying desperately not to inflict herself into the lives of her adult children. And as Colin remembered from his childhood, Grandma Kitty did quite well for herself and Raymie. Kitty had a real knack in the kitchen, with sewing and other useful crafts. One year, when Raymie was about to start kindergarten, Kitty was hired at the middle school just two blocks from her house to be the assistant to the Home Economics teacher. Class sizes were big, middle schoolers weren't the easiest to corral and the long-time Home Ec teacher was having medical issues. Kitty and Ms. Rainmaker got along just fine. Ms. R. gave Kitty the toughest kids and gave her lots of leeway to keep those kids involved and on task. Kitty loved the work and loved the kids (it was mutual). Kitty's pay and benefits along with Joe's pension and a little Social Security kept Raymie and her independent and "respectable". Ms. R. missed a lot of school. The administration never called in a sub and Kitty "played teacher" doing a great job. When Ms. R. had to take a disability retirement in the middle of the school year, somehow the school district got "dispensation" so that Kitty who had no degree or even a college credit to her name, could stay on as teacher for many years.

During those early years in Raymie and Colin's lives, the boys spent a lot of time together since they were always in the same elementary school classrooms. Ruth and Kitty shared childcare, food stamps, vacations and lots of other simple pieces of their lives. Gil, Ruth's husband, was father and surrogate father to the boys and although Colin never had a brother or sister, Raymie filled the bill and life was good. The boys, nephew and uncle, were more like cousins, brothers, friends. They didn't live near each other, but they had bikes, the streets were safe and there was always a caring adult to keep things copacetic.

Then Ray met Anna... or was it Brenda, or maybe it was Carol. Ray had what Colin called the ABC wives. Colin always wondered if Ray was purposefully working his way through the alphabet. It was possible that it was the BCA wives or the CBA wives but, whatever it was, Colin could easily remember their names by thinking ABC... Anna, Brenda, Carol. There were just three. Perhaps Ray had given up on being married or he just couldn't find a D out there that suited him.

When Ray met Anna they were still in high school. Immediately after throwing those mortar boards in the air, they were in Vegas: married, waiting tables, floor show dancing, couch jumping, gambling and then divorced. Anna stayed with "a new man" while Ray came home and to Kitty's great joy he worked and went to the community college. It was the same community college where Colin had just about finished with an associate degree and was ready to transfer to a four-year school.

Then Ray met Brenda… or was it Carol, or maybe it was Anna. They both studied criminal justice. They soon moved to some town in North Carolina that paid for a program in criminal justice at their local vocational-technical college if the students promised to stay on for at least a two year stint in their regional police force. According to Ray's letters to Grandma Kitty, the two fledgling officers were doing well. They were happy with the surroundings, considering marriage, eventually having kids and working on their bachelor degrees in criminal justice.

Colin postponed the BA degree and spent four years in the US Navy instead. He met Veronica Jackson when he resumed his college education as a junior just down the road at Fredonia State College. They each had stops and starts with getting serious about a college education. At the beginning of the fall semester in their senior year, they found themselves in a "kiddie lit" course that all elementary education majors had to take. During their extended "gap years", there had been jobs, Colin's four year stint in the US Navy, and a semi-serious romance or two for each of them. All that time, Vonny, as she preferred to be called, had been saving for college. Colin utilized the GI Bill to pay his tuition. Early in the that fall semester, the "kiddie lit" teacher paired students together and assigned them to write a children's book that featured two characters having a dialogue where a value was clarified. Little did that professor realize that when he paired Colin and Vonny for that short-term assignment that he had in reality paired them for life. Colin much preferred solo assignments, but what was he to do? He and Vonny met for a planning session in the student union and almost immediately, as Colin would later say… "Sparks flew. She couldn't resist me!" The story book assignment loomed at the top of their syllabus requirements with them both being serious students. The mixing and matching of studying, dating, creating and canoodling led to "Gertie Gets a Friend". Their story centered around two witches dealing with honesty issues as they repaired bicycles for the children in their neighborhood. Both authors were pleased with the final results and Vonny even created several drawings to accompany their text. Their story was voted the class favorite by their classroom peers so Colin and Vonny got to share it with preschool students at the on-campus day care center for the children of staff members.

Colin and Vonny got married on spring break in their senior year. It was then possible for them to live in married student housing as they started work on their master degrees right after their May graduations. It was a small family wedding in the gazebo in Grandma Kitty's back yard with Kitty and Ruth and Vonny's mom catering a grand picnic dinner for the thirty or so invited guests. Pastor Gordon,

Kitty's eldest boy, officiated. Ray and Brenda, (or Carol or Anna), could not get away from work in North Carolina to attend, but they did send nice monogrammed towels from a department store in their area. The accompanying card invited Colin and Vonny to drop in "any ole time".

The reverse happened. One day Colin came home from an early class to find Ray fast asleep in a chair on the small porch of their just-big-enough-for-two married student apartment. Ray explained that his job was boring, he hated security patrols at the county courthouse, and his relationship was a bust. Brenda, or whoever, remained in school and on the police force down south. "She is there for good," said Ray.

Colin knew a senior who had a place off-campus. He had just lost a roommate so Ray moved in, paid rent, became a part-time student and learned to enjoy college life in a small town. Fortunately, most of Ray's North Carolina college credits transferred north so when Colin received his MA in Education and Vonny received her MA in Social Work (after a program change from Elementary Education), Ray got a BA in Criminal Justice. Grandma Kitty, Ruth and Vonny's mom outdid themselves with a picnic celebration for the multiple graduates. Family and friends congregated for a splendid celebration! Announcements were made: Colin took a teaching job in Jamestown; Vonny was expecting a child in February; Ray was headed to Baltimore, Maryland to become part of an inner-city police tactical unit.

Life went on as it has a way of doing and as happens too, Colin and Ray grew apart. There was a card or two and that terrible funeral situation, but during the last nearly twenty years, there had been little family interaction with Ray and no congregating like that three-fold college graduation party.

Life in general, work and home and community went well for the O'Briens. Ronny, Colin and Vonny's first child, was soon joined by Jackson, Jack for short, and then along came Erin Elizabeth to complete their family.

As a result of Ray's telephone call and his impending arrival, a flood of childhood memories filled Colin's mind as he held on tight to the calm of his thinking place on the foot-bridge over the Maple Springs Creek. All those thoughts were soon crowded out by projections of the current, unsettling, unknown, immediate future days that would follow the arrival "next door" "tomorrow" of Uncle Ray.

CHAPTER 2

"Tomorrow," answered Colin. He had certainly fore-seen that question.

"Tomorrow?" said Vonny mid-pace in the kitchen. "Oh Colin, Colin, Colin. Oh Ray, Ray, Ray."

Pacing continued. Sputtering ceased. Vonny moved out onto the porch that had just recently been painted and decorated. She plopped herself into a white wicker rocker and directed her energy into the rocking mode that suited her frame of mind. Colin gave her a few minutes and when he detected that the rocking rate had lessened, he headed out onto the porch with a bottle of Chardonnay and two wine glasses.

Vonny clutched a pillow, but released her strangle hold to take a wine glass. Colin poured for her, poured again for himself and then sat.

Colin was certain that he had given Vonny sufficient information when he blurted out to her that Ray was to be expected. Colin had easily mentioned who, why, even the where and the when, but he knew that it was the "when" that had been a tough pill to swallow. He had reassured Vonny that their summer plans remained intact and that Ray would not be a pest. Colin also said something that he had not rehearsed; he thought Ray was surely a different person who needed a break, "let's take the high road and give him that chance."

"I know it's a shock," said Colin, "but perhaps it's better to have little or no notification of his arrival rather than to have an arrival time set weeks ahead and then to have all that time to worry about his showing up. You know, stew about it. I'm just surprised that he's to be right next door, in Brian's place, and that Brian didn't even email or call us about it. Maybe Ray didn't tell him we're related. Who knows?"

Colin and Vonny sat silently for a moment each mapping their own high road.

"I know," said Vonny. Then after another long pause, "Brian sent me a text a couple of days ago. Said for you to call him. I forgot to tell you. If you had a cell phone, then he could call or text you and I wouldn't have to be your secretary."

"I'll call him now," said Colin navigating a different high road. He got up and went into the house to use the land line, a cordless telephone, that was in its cradle on the kitchen counter.

Brian picked up after the first ring. "Brian. It's Colin in The Springs. Sorry that I didn't get back to you sooner. Guess I got busy. How're you doin? What's new?"

"Colin, my man. Good to hear your voice," said Brian sounding energetic. "Sorry that I haven't been a better long-distance friend, but it's been a busy winter. I've been in New Zealand a couple times and in fact, we, Kelly and

Mindy and I, are spending the summer there and that's why our cottage was available for the entire season. Wasn't it a gas that your uncle found our place on *Craig's List*. And he's probably enroute as we speak. He's a great guy, very independent considering that he's totally blind. He's to be admired."

"Blind?" Colin asked.

CHAPTER 3

"Blind?" Vonny asked.

"Blind," replied Colin. "Brian's met Ray and has been working with him so that he'd be safe here. Let me tell you all that Brian shared. We'll probably get more details when we have our heart-to-heart with Ray. Brian assumed that Ray had called us. I didn't tell him otherwise, but I did plead innocent saying that I didn't know that Ray is blind. Brian didn't tell me Ray's story, just how he'd helped Ray make sure it would all work out here.

"Ray contacted Brian via email after he found Brian's place listed under 'cottage rentals/east coast' on *Craig's List*. Then they talked a few times and even met for coffee in Baltimore. They live not too far apart and Ray had learned the transit system and so he went to Brian's house once. Oh yeah, blind. Ray was blinded a little over a year ago when he was shot 'in the line of duty'. According to Brian, Ray told him that he has been to what he called 'blind school' and he is pretty independent. He uses a cane well and he uses it all the time because sight impaired people have to really be proficient with a cane before they will be considered ready for a help dog.

"Listen to this! Brian created a floor plan of the cottage and printed it on a 3D printer and so it is embossed-like and Ray reads it like Braille and now he knows where everything is in the house and he'll be able to navigate the house independently. Brian went the extra mile and made a 3D map of the bulk of Maple Springs so that Ray can go for a walk by himself and not get lost. Kelly connected Ray with Eileen. Eileen's opening up the place and she's available for any needed repairs and she's organized meals from Vicki at *Elegant Edibles* in Jamestown. Eileen also has one of the Amish girls in Wally's family coming in to clean once a week. There, you got it all. I almost forgot to tell you that Brian, Kelly and Mindy are spending the summer in New Zealand, for Brian's work, tech stuff, so that's why their cottage is available for the whole summer. Ya good?"

Vonny was good. She had taken it all in, it made sense, it sounded like it was something to embrace.

"I'm on the high road honey," was Vonny's response to Colin.

Just then a small truck, a Tacoma, came down the street. It stopped in front of the O'Brien's porch, it actually pulled on to the lawn a bit, and then out of the driver's window came the top half of Eileen Miller, property manager extraordinaire.

"Hello O'Briens. Howya doin'?" said Eileen. "Brian, next door, just texted me to remind me to get the doors unlocked and the windas open to his house for his summer-long tenant. Says he's yer uncle. Yer blind uncle. That right?"

"Hi Eileen. Yep, that's right. Ray is my mom's brother.

He surprised us with this cottage situation, but looks like it's all a done deal and it'll probably be fun. You need help with anything?" asked Colin.

"Got 'er," said Eileen and she was gone. Colin and Vonny watched her turn the corner and heard her stop in Brian's driveway which ran between the two houses and then they heard the driver's door open and slam shut. Eileen was the "brawn of The Springs"; she either personally performed or organized the performance of dock and cottage maintenance for the majority of the Springers. It was obvious that she was on the clock for Brian.

"I saw her there a couple times this week, early in the morning," Vonny said. "I thought she was opening up for Brian."

"She's thorough. The place is probably ready. I hope she didn't rearrange the furniture," said Colin with a big grin on his face.

"Colin, you are terrible," said Vonny. Her cell phone rang and she slipped it out of her blouse pocket. "Hello. Ronny, hon. What's up? Everything's all right, isn't it?" Vonny rocked, talked, laughed and made faces at Colin then disconnected after making kissing noises into the phone.

"Ronny says everything is a go, she's running late. So what else is new? They won't be here until next weekend. They have to be at the college early in the morning for paperwork and orientation and so they are going right there tomorrow. Dan has meetings and lessons right away Monday morning. They want to get to know the other grad students and the campus. We won't see them until next Friday night for dinner. Darn."

After plopping herself on Colin's lap and giving him quick kisses, Vonny went inside to change her clothes. Colin poured himself more wine, pulled closer a footstool so as to make it useful and thought about the summer weekends that had been planned through a series of phone and email messages between Vonny and the three kids. Ronny and Dan would be around every weekend and the other two along with their mates would be around now and then during the summer.

Ronny and Dan were to be at Fredonia State College, twenty-three miles away door-to-door, studying during an eight-week summer session. Ronny was working on a Behavior Analyst Certificate and Dan was serving as the percussion instructor for eight, week-long marching band camps. They would be working during the weekdays and then have the weekends free. They'd be in The Springs on the weekends for meals, relaxing and laundry duties. They'd be around to celebrate their first wedding anniversary too. Last summer, in what turned out to be a three day party, they were married with lots of friends and family hanging out for the duration. Vonny had arranged everything, but Colin had been in charge of housing. Housing consisted of renting eight cottages, situating six tents scattered on lawns along with the rental of several port-a-johns and at least four trailers carefully positioned on neighbors' driveways. A series of grills in a separate tent facilitated meals; guests brought lots to share while careful coordination with area caterers assured that there was more than enough to eat and drink for all three days. The weather was perfect for the wedding and for two or three days pre and post. Ronny was a gorgeous bride. She wore Vonny's wedding dress that she had altered. It was shortened and scooped at the neck to suit her own style. Dan wore tan pants with a white, formal, linen Guayabera shirt. Dan looked ever the island gentleman, serene and confident. Jack and Erin attended and Colin gave away his darling daughter. Vonny, mainly, cried. All in all it was a perfect three days: calm waters, bright sun, a lake breeze, mimosas, campfires, sing-a-longs, star filled skies, lots of PDsA. This past year flew right by! This summer, number five at the lake, was sure to do the same.

CHAPTER 4

Colin woke up to voices talking right outside his bedroom window. He soon realized that it was Vonny talking with someone whose voice he did not recognize. It was more laughing than talking, but then, that was Vonny. Colin loved that about her. She truly enjoyed people. She was a great listener and she smiled, laughed, even sparkled almost in excess.

"Quiet down out there. How's a fella to get any sleep around here?" Colin yelled through the curtains and window screen while he slipped on khaki shorts and a bright blue t-shirt with Alfred E. Newman's "What me worry?" face on the front. Vonny hated that shirt.

"Get out here Colin. Sally Mitchell's here. Come on, move it."

"Coming!" Colin yelled through the kitchen window as he quickly, sloppily, poured himself a cup of coffee and headed out the back door. Colin greeted the ladies and they easily fell into laughing and gabbing over the fence that separated the O'Brien property from Uncle Ray's summer digs, Brian and Kelly Jensen's cottage.

Sally Mitchell and Vonny had been neighbors as little girls and spent twelve years together in the Jamestown Public School system. They often crossed paths both socially and professionally after high school.

"What brings you to Maple Springs, to our 'beauty spot on Lake Chautauqua'?" asked Colin.

"Hi Colin. Long time no see," said Sally. "I still work for the Blind Association as their mobilization expert, although I am the only one that puts the word 'expert' after the word 'mobilization', and I'm here to meet Raymond McGill. He said he'd be in residence by 10:00 this morning."

"We're expecting him too," said Colin. "We didn't have any specific time, but I'm sure that he'll be along. Come over for coffee. We'll hear any car that drives up."

And just then, onto the Jensen property, drove a long, sleek, white limousine. Horn beeping ensued. It was good that Sally had parked her Honda in the street because the limo hogged the entire paved, narrow driveway. Two men in dark suits and white shirts, both sporting sunglasses, emerged from the car looking like the Blues Brothers ready to burst into song.

"Colin old pal. Great to see you. I brought you a present: a blast from your past, a brother from another mother. You know this guy, Uncle Ray," said Bill Morris, limo driver and a long-time friend of Colin's. Bill moved around the car and offered a guide arm to Ray and the two of them joined the trio at the fence.

"Colin," said Ray. "It's been a while. How'm I lookin'? Bill says you're doin' great. Would 'e lie? Mornin' ladies. I know you're lookin' good Vonny, Bill told me that emphatically."

For a few seconds the five adults just stood there, each mind trying to fit together scattered pieces that hallmarked the assemblage. Then Colin, ever the master of ceremonies and the social maven, made all the necessary introductions. Everyone was charming. The chill was even off the smile and greeting that Vonny gave to Ray. The quick social amenities ended and Sally excused herself and Ray as they moved to the cottage's back door with Sally guiding and commentarying as they entered.

"That guy has a solid grasp on life, I'd say," said Bill to Colin and Vonny. "I picked him up at the Greyhound Bus Station in Erie He sat up front, and we, or really mostly he, talked all the way here. He's excited to be here and see you two. Said he never met your kids. How'd that happen? Gotta go! I have a pick up at the Chautauqua Institution in nineteen minutes and it's a fifteen minute ride from here. Wish me luck. I'll be around. Bye."

Bill popped his trunk, put one huge, black suitcase, a black backpack and what looked like a guitar case on the front porch. Then Bill was off down the street and out of sight. He had just used one of those precious minutes that he had between the fifteen that he needed and the nineteen that he had to work with.

The mini-flash mob that had just assembled now only consisted of Vonny and Colin.

"I'm off to Skillman's. They are having a 'Welcome to Summer Sale'. I'll be home for supper. You're on duty," said

Vonny. "I'll be bushed. Shopping takes all the energy I have. Love you. Ditch that shirt. Hate it!"

With that quick encapsulation of her day, her feelings and her likes and dislikes, Vonny was in the car, out of the driveway and quickly out of sight, but not at her former lead-footed pace. A couple traffic tickets in the recent past had partially quashed her propensity for speed.

Colin, ever the creative one, moved to his recycling bin and "dove" for tin cans (they were probably aluminum). He got busy at his small, make-shift workbench in his crowded Amish shed at the head of the driveway. The cans were clean because he always washed recyclables before plopping them in his no-sort recycle bin. He punched a hole in the intact end of each can and connected them with a piece of white cotton string which he had cut to a length of about 50 feet. He secured the string and then hung one can and the majority of the string on the fence near where the flash mob had just met. He then popped the screen on one of his small, three-in-a-row kitchen windows and put the other can and about five feet of string into his kitchen. He was sure that the cans would get used even if it was just for today, but the apparatus would surely engender a laugh and a flashback into the childhood days of Colin and Raymie.

Colin went quickly into the house and, ever the good sailor, took a navy shower and quickly dressed. He came outside and hopped onto his newest summer-time luxury, a deep blue beach bike complete with basket. He pedaled off to Steve's Store for the good early morning pickin's of fresh produce brought to the outdoor bins by local Amish farmers. The slow-to-rise or habitual afternoon shopper had to settle for small tomatoes, wrinkled cukes and other slightly off-color or misshapen produce items. Colin left the store with a lot of plump, colorful, bright, firm pieces of produce sure to be enjoyed during the next few days.

Once home, Colin quickly washed, dried, partially peeled and then carefully and evenly sliced two just-purchased medium-sized eggplants. He liked to call them les aubergines just to be funny. He then submerged the slices into salted water. He'd dry them and then egg and breadcrumb them before frying to make "eggplant stackers", a real favorite in the O'Brien household.

Just then the newly installed communication device "rang" and startled Colin.

"You have reached the O'Brien household. Sorry we can't come to the can just now," said Colin loudly with great enunciation into the devise. "Leave a message and we will shout back at you as soon as we CAN." The can vibrated with laughter as Colin exited the house and met Ray and Sally at Ray's end of that newly devised communication system.

"This should be an interesting summer here with the two of you in Maple Springs," said Sally as she took the can from Ray and replaced it on the fence. "You two guys enjoy yourselves. I will see you early tomorrow Ray. Be sure to wear your sneakers; we have lots of ground to cover. Bye guys."

"So. Ray. You good? What d'ya need? Ya got food? Where's your glasses? Your stuff? I can move anything for ya. Tell me to shut up," said Colin as Sally sprinted to her car. Almost immediately Colin felt the need to stifle himself by placing a hand over his mouth.

"Colin. I got it. I been studying the house plan that Brian gave me. I packed my own bags so I know everything I have and now I even know where it all is thanks to Sally's help. And I don't usually wear dark glasses. Vicki something from *Elegant Edibles* stopped by with food. I don't know where you were. She went to your house to say hello, but you weren't there. She brought me lots of staples and some salads already in zip-lock bags. She made main meals ahead and wrapped them in different products, so as long as I remember what's in Tupperware, what's in Corning Ware, what's in styrofoam and what's in tin foil, I can actually have the meals I want on the days I want them. No guesswork as long as I avoid amnesia and dementia. I know that the Corning Ware is vegetarian lasagna and I'd like it if you and Vonny would come over tonight and share it with me. Possible?"

It was possible. Les aubergines stacks could wait. It might be best to grab this uncle by the horns to set the proper tone for the summer.

"Vonny is shopping, but should be home soon. We

will be at your door at 5:30, apple pie in hand." said Colin. "Beer, right?"

Ray extended a hand ready for shaking. Colin took it and happily shook it.

"Beer goes great with lasagna, but none for me. See ya when ya show." Ray made a smart turn and with his white, red tipped cane in hand leading the way, he made it gracefully to the two steps into the back door of his summer home. He stepped up those two steps as though he had made that move a thousand times before and was out of sight, gone into the kitchen looking for that Corning Ware dish containing supper for three.

Vonny returned tired, as she said she would be, and gave Colin a mini-fashion show of the new, "on-sale" items that jumped off the rack into her arms. By 5:30 the O'Briens were taking the high road to Ray McGill's summer retreat on Lake Chautauqua, next door, pie in hand.

CHAPTER 5

Colin stood on the foot-bridge over the Maple Springs Creek looking upstream. This was twice in as many days that he had had to employ the solitude of his thinking place; once before the arrival of Uncle Ray and now the second occurrence to think through that arrival and the heart-to-heart that had materialized as Ray had promised.

This heart-to-heart had really been more of a mind-to-mind and a gut-to-gut conversation. Ray was prepared for this moment, this long awaited event. Colin thought that Ray might have even done some rehearsing of salient topics that he did not want avoided or to be left out of the conversation entirely. Colin noticed that there was no apologizing either. He did not expect an apology, or a litany of reasons for some of Ray's actions (or inactions) over the years, and that's just what he got. No apology, no rehash of hurts or slights or ignoring that Ray had foisted onto his family and friends. Ray had regrets, druthers and embarrassments that he chronicled. In all the recounting of issues by Ray, it was obvious that he was the most hurt, the most deprived and the obvious loser. Colin was soon sure that there had been a rehearsal and perhaps even work done with a counselor or life coach whose aim it was to help make Ray "whole" again. Ray probably also wanted to give solace to the folks that he had hurt, ignored, demeaned or wronged. Colin said very little. Vonny was silent. Although at one time Vonny, Colin, Ray and an A, B or C were friends and were all supportive of each other individually and as couples, Vonny's social work training prevailed and she let the "client" talk.

Before Colin and Vonny left Ray's and hustled home, Vonny had hugged Ray. First she grabbed his hand and almost dragged him to his feet and then she performed a long, full body hug. Colin followed suit and the O'Briens left voicing "thanks, good night, we'll continue this talk, see you tomorrow".

"I am so glad that we used disposable dishes," said Vonny. "I'd have been guilty as could be if I had left poor Ray with a mess to clean up."

"Don't call him poor Ray," said Colin as he shut their bedroom window that looked out onto their side yard and the backdoor of Ray's cottage. He then drew the flowered drapes that matched the bedspread.

"He's Ray, an old friend found again and he's trying to introduce some control into this next piece of his life. He was on, I'd say. He ran through years of his actions which obviously rematerialized during sessions of personal reflection. I'd say he had some counseling sessions, betcha at blind school. Stuff he mentioned and included on his list of hurts that I am sure he thought were hurtful to me, I don't even remember. Some of those items, like the Christmas when Ronny was one and we had her Christened at midnight mass and he didn't attend even though he was in town, I remember, but it wasn't a big deal. Lots of stuff. Grandma's funeral had him on the ropes. I could hear it in his voice. Wow, that was intense and I kept wanting to chime in and sooth or forgive or something, but I didn't want to stop his momentum. Yikes, he's here for less than twelve hours and he's revisited over thirty years of what I'm sure he'd call his litany of gaffs."

Colin sat on the edge of the bed, but made no efforts to get ready for bed. Vonny was quick in her efforts to "get prone".

"I'm closing up and will bring in the porch cushions. Rain, I think," said Colin and by the time he accomplished those things and came back to the bedroom, Vonny was fast asleep. He decided to take a quick walk, it was early, hardly dark. Colin wasn't surprised that he ended up at his thinking place.

Colin bounced a bit using his leg muscles to get the foot-bridge to also bounce a bit and he did his habitual scan of upstream and the banks on the sides of the creek before he turned to the west to check out the evening sky. It wasn't the night sky just yet, although the sun had slunk behind the horizon. There was still a sky full of exposed color. It was nine o'clock. Colin knew this because he could hear the chimes on the Miller Bell Tower at Chautauqua Institution across the lake. The O'Briens positioned their dock, the last dock at the end of what was the northern end of the Maple

Springs Bay, to point directly at Chautauqua Institution. Colin had seen a vintage, hand-drawn map that had a line drawn from the position of their dock to the Bell Tower that gave the distance as 2.2 miles. He fancied that one day he would swim that route, probably just one way.

Colin was quickly comforted by his place and his thinking revolved around the evolution of Ray McGill. Although Ray's review of the past thirty-plus years of his personal life was cursory, he didn't hedge when relating his scurrilous life style. There was little mention of benevolent actions or commendable community or professional activities. The negative activities and interactions with others chronicled by Ray would hardly have left him time to be gracious, positive or beneficent. Alcohol(ism) was the prevailing item (activity) and Ray was circumspect in relating how all pervasive that lifestyle was in creating Ray, the flawed police detective, the miserable human being. Colin could not fathom how Ray functioned, especially at work, when he was highly involved with and enthralled by "the bottle". "The bottle" was how Ray described his long-term association with spirits, booze, drink, alcohol. Apparently too there had been periods of sobriety. Although Ray did not say so, those time were probably police department initiated.

Needless to say, the hold of "the bottle" had kept Ray from other more positive activities that would have suited a man of Ray's skills and potential. In the year since he was blinded, Ray had been a "work in progress" and Colin thought Ray was working hard at being a new person, an honest and caring person.

The result of overactive thinking had engulfed Colin and he was soon aware of the arrival of the night sky. He hurried home. As he slid into bed, he had to move Vonny over to her half. He initiated spooning and was soon asleep, taken there by warm childhood flashes of two silly boys t-p-ing a porch, riding bikes over plywood jumps and lobbing crab apples at billboards.

CHAPTER 6

Vonny was up early on Sunday morning and gone to St. Timothy's Lutheran Church to be a guest speaker concerning spirituality and the nursing home resident. St. Tim's had a committee that organized their visiting of shut-ins and nursing home residents and the group was growing in number and offerings. Vonny had spoken to the committee and was glad to return a second time to talk to the entire church congregation. Colin was up for breakfast with her, but decided not to join her at church. He had heard the talk several times. Vonny always spoke well. Instead, Colin continued the work that he and Vonny had begun in the garden. Lots to do, but Colin had carefully put the yard to sleep in the fall and waking her up in the spring was not the chore that fall-lazy gardeners might experience. The O'Briens had flats of flowers to place lovingly in decorative pots here and there on the porch and even in the gardens. Colin loved what he called "garden furniture", statuary and pots interspersed with in-ground plants. He was anxious to get flowers potted and statuary placed. The in-ground flowers and ground cover was about 95% perennial plants and those hearty little devils had quickly popped back to life. Colin loved spring, loved to see his neighborhood renewed. He had gotten a late start on the garden this year, but was sure he'd get the chance to enjoy his labors into the early fall.

Colin was just coming outside to work in the garden when he saw Ray and Sally heading off at a quick pace away from Ray's, down Lakeview Avenue toward the lake. It looked like Ray was ready to test out his ability to walk The Springs after he had studied the 3D neighborhood map that Brian had created. Ray was using his cane and Sally was next to him, not guiding him, but talking at the same quick pace that she was walking. During Colin's early morning garden foray, he saw Ray and Sally walking down close-by streets at a quick pace. He kept to himself not wanting to interrupt what he was sure had to be serious instruction on Sally's part. He thought too that it probably wasn't often that the Blind Association's Mobilization Expert worked on a Sunday morning.

The late morning sun was starting to bake Colin and he thought that he'd take a break and have a cold drink. He went into the house and quickly made a pitcher of his favorite hot weather drink, half and half of iced tea and lemonade. He took the pitcher on a tray with plastic cups and placed it on the small wrought iron table on the porch at Ray's. Colin was sure that Ray and Sally had to be heating up too and they'd surely appreciate a cold drink once Sally had stopped cracking the whip. Or was it Ray who was dragging Sally around The Springs? Colin hadn't seen them in a while. They must have traveled beyond the boundaries of the map that Brian had created. Colin sat in a comfortable folding chair with an added cushion that Eileen must have placed on the front porch when she was opening up the Jensen's cottage for Ray. The walking duo would be along soon and Colin hoped to join them for a cold drink.

The Jensen's porch was not in the sun in the morning, but heated right up in the afternoon because it faced west. The porch was originally enclosed, but the Jensens had it opened-up and it was inviting. The best feature of the porch was that it had a great view of the lake when one was looking directly down Forest Lawn Avenue. The porch had no railings except at the stairs. There were potted geraniums placed at two corners. Colin noticed that there was now square molding around the edge of the porch, except where the stairs met the porch floor. It was probably nailed there by Eileen to help Ray to enjoy the porch and not have to worry that a chair might be back just a bit too far and slip off the edge and onto the ground. Just as Colin got comfortable, Ray and Sally came into view and were definitely going at a slower pace, perhaps in the cool down phase of their forced march.

"Hey, Colin," called Sally. "You look like you're guarding the place. I thought The Springs was a friendly place. I told Ray that we didn't have to lock the door."

"We are all safe here. I am not a guard. I am the welcome home committee. I brought cold drinks. What d' ya' say?"

"Colin, save me from this slave driver," said Ray as his

cane touched the bottom step and he quickly grabbed the railing. He got himself to the porch floor and stepped forward and to the right and let his cane find him a chair. He approached the chair, then he turned and sank into it with pathetic, fake sounds of exhaustion.

"Grow up, buddy boy," said Sally. "Gotta go! I have a quick meeting with a family just down the road in Hartfield and I will be back by one o'clock. We're doing Broadway and Summit."

"Not the hills, no please, not the hills," said Ray as he slid from the chair to his knees and begged Sally for mercy.

"Colin, have a heart-to-heart with this guy. Someone has to be an adult around here."

By now they were all laughing. Colin poured drinks and they all sat for the moment, got a breath and enjoyed the shade of the porch.

"Gotta go guys. See you at 1:00, Ray. Bye. Want to join us, Colin?" said Sally as she left the porch and got into her car that was in the driveway. As she backed out of the driveway and headed sedately down the street, Vonny came from the opposite direction and her car refilled the driveway and she joined the guys on the porch.

"You just missed Sally, Hon," said Colin. "But she'll be back by one o'clock. Won't she Ray?"

"She's a task master. She'll be back. I'll be ready. More lemonade please," said Ray. "Where ya been Vonny?"

Vonny told of her venture at St. Timothy's church and

that was the discussion for a moment. Colin told of his gardening endeavors and his plans for his next encounter with his perennial friends. Ray was silent for a moment and then stood at his chair.

"Stay right where you are guys. I have something to show you and a bit of a continuation of the trajectory that I started to lay out last night. I'll be right back. Mother nature beckons," said Ray as he hurried seamlessly into the house, except for the screen door hitting him in the butt as he went in the door too slowly.

By the time Colin poured Vonny a drink and he told her about Ray and Sally's morning activities, Ray was back with a large manila envelope. He sat, emptied the contents of the envelope onto his lap and began to talk.

"This is a picture of Deanna."

Vonny took the picture from Ray and turned it so that she and Colin could both see it.

"She's coming to visit this coming Saturday," continued Ray. "I didn't talk much about blind school last night, but it was a great experience. I learned a lot while I was there. I can't imagine navigating in this world without the tools they provided. I met Deanna there. She is an OT person, an intuitive nurse and practitioner with ideas galore. I know and you know that they tell you not to get involved with people that you meet in rehab, but this rehab isn't like other rehabs that I've been privileged to attend and Deanna is not like the people I met at other rehabs. This organization I don't even call rehab, nor do they. I say that I'm reconditioned. You know, like a car gets reconditioned and it's better than ever with new souped-up features."

"She's quite lovely. Is this a recent picture? How did you know that that was her picture that you passed to us?" asked Vonny.

"Yes, it's new. It's a selfie. I thought that I should have pictures of my visitors so that you all could be apprised of who's showing up, who you need to be nice to. There are only two 8 x 10 pictures in this envelope and the one of Deanna has a bent corner. The other photo, of Adam and his daughter, does not. Adam is a personal trainer and he is coming to visit too. He's bringing a van of equipment and Deanna and his daughter, Tori." Ray held the second picture out and Vonny took it too.

"Oh, so that's the impetus for all the exercise. Adam is coming and you don't want to be winded when he puts you to work," said Colin.

"No," said Ray. "I haven't slacked off a day since I started with him. I just want to really know this place so that we don't waste time with me bumbling around The Springs. Adam is a former cop too. He got injured a couple years ago and when he was doing rehab, he liked the discipline so much that he didn't come back to the force. Instead, he started his own business. He has three people working for him. He has done lots of work rehabbing injured cops who are trying to get back to street duty so that they don't get stuck behind a desk.

"Anyway, let me tell you about Deanna…," started Ray.

"Holy macaroni!" shouted Colin as he jumped to his feet. "You got your D! You know Anna, Brenda, Carol, A B C, and now Deanna, D!"

"Colin, you've been in the sun too much this morning. What're you going on about?" said Vonny.

Colin could hardly settle so that he could relate to Ray and Vonny about his wife-name-remembering mnemonic device…the ABC trio and now the ABCD quartet. Ray and Vonny enjoyed Colin's slide into his strange little world of humor, but not as much as Colin did.

Vonny then insisted that the trio discuss next Friday's arrivals and what might have to be organized to make everything work out. "There will be eight of us," she said.

"Make that nine," said Ray. I almost forgot to mention that Deanna has a daughter, Kenzie. She's the same age as Tori, 16, and she's joining us too. All four of them will be here from late Thursday night until Sunday afternoon. I gotta know this house and The Springs by the time they get here. Vicki's gonna bring staples, you know bread, eggs, peanut butter, cereal and some meat ready for grillin' and a big pot of chili. We'll get some wings and pizza delivered and we'll be fine. You gotta meet these guys. Don't be scared or ignore us. We're here on vacation. We're lookin' for nothin' special."

"Ray, Ray, slow down, you are making me nervous.

Four more people, food, beds to make...," began Colin.

"Colin!" said Vonny perhaps too loudly. "This man has a plan AND everyone that's coming can take care of themselves, chip in to get things done and they all know each other. Relax, will ya?"

"Ray," Vonny started talking again after everyone took a deep breath. "The weekend sounds great. It's too early for many of the Springers to be returning to their cottages, so it will still be quiet around here. Perfect time for getting acclimated. And here's some good news. Ronny and her husband Dan, two more people to add to your new cadre of friends, will be here this weekend and every weekend for the next eight weeks actually. Jack and Erin will be around this summer too. Are you sure that you are ready for all this family? And speaking of family, there's a raft of siblings and nieces and nephews out there that, believe it or not, I am sure would like to see you. No pressure, we'll plan something for later and not subject Deanna, Adam and the girls to all those kin just yet."

"Steady as she goes," said Ray. "Give me air. We'll talk. I gotta have some lunch. Sally will be back soon and if I don't eat, I'll pass out half-way up the Broadway Street hill."

"I can fix that," said Vonny as she jumped up and went to her car. She came back with a plate of finger sandwiches, made with bread tinted in pastel colors, no crusts; it was egg salad and tuna salad sandwiches that had been left over from the after-church-service-coffee-hour at St. Tim's.

Colin refilled glasses with his tea/lemonade drink and the three reacquainted friends enjoyed the lunch and the company and chatted casually about the upcoming week-end. Soon Ray went into the house to do some stretching so that he was relimbered for Sally. Vonny drove home eager for a quick change out of her church-going outfit and Colin walked home with a tray of lunch leftovers wondering what the afternoon would bring.

CHAPTER 7

The afternoon was spent at the water's edge, but not in a relaxed mode as one usually thinks of when someone spends time "at the shore". The O'Briens were instead in work mode. They cleaned kayaks and set up chairs and a small fire pit. By 3:00 the green, plastic Adirondack chairs were occupied and the late afternoon sun was proving therapeutic. Vonny's cell phone sang its sweet answer-me-song, *Dancing Queen*, and she grabbed it from its safe position on a small table between the chairs away from the water's edge.

"Hello," sang Vonny. "Oh, hi Benny. Yes, Mother Nature is cooperating. It's mid-June and we're at the dock, enjoying the sun." Vonny failed to mention the two hours that she and Colin had just devoted to kayak cleaning. "How's Christine? Hope she's planning on resuming Tai Chi. We'll start up again after July 4th. She can join in when you two get here."

Vonny spent the next couple of minutes just listening, making sounds that indicated that she was commiserating, or at least listening, and then she said, "Oh Benny, you best tell all this to Colin. I'll mess up the translating. I'll give the phone to him. Tell Christine hello." Vonny handed the phone to Colin, indicated that she had to go home for a minute and hurried away leaving Colin to deal with Benny Strand. Benny was a neighbor a couple of doors down, across the street, who summered in Maple Springs but who spent winter months in a non-winter-like place, Fort Pierce, Florida.

"Hi Benny. Colin here. What was it that Vonny was so worried about translating?" With that opening, Benny, calling from his southern domicile, began a story and completed his end of the conversation by asking for a favor or two.

Colin responded appropriately from his Maple Springs' end of the conversation and pushed the button on the phone to end the call. Hanging up and sometimes initiating a call was the extent of Colin's familiarity with the cell phone. He neither wanted nor needed a cell phone. Well, one had come in handy several times in the last couple years, but he certainly didn't care to be at everyone's beck and call. A couple years earlier when he had been temporarily deputized by the local sheriff, he was grateful for Vonny's cell phone that was in the glove compartment of her car when he needed to inform the sheriff where a possible murderer was hiding out. Recently he only used the cell phone to take messages regarding wedding plan specifics for Ronny and Dan wedding last summer.

"Did you get all that?" said Vonny as she returned to her chair and opened a canvas bag and took out some Switchback beer, a gift from son Jack. She also had a container with Havarti cheese and some round, salt free crackers. The cheese was from down the road at the cheese factory in Dewittville, Cadwell's, and the crackers were from Aldi's; "splurge on the cheese, the crackers aren't important".

"Yes m'dear. I got it all. No problem. Kaitlin Strand is getting married, early August, and so they won't be around till the middle of that month. First daughter and all, they are hammered with things to do. You know Christine, she is highly involved. The wedding is in their yard. Yes, they have a tent. So there is housework, yardwork and wedding-work. No wonder we won't see them till it's all over. He said that they be staying through September and probably into October. The main reason he called is to tell us that he rented out their house here, you know, "The Landing", and he'd like us to keep an eye on it. He emphasized that we were not to engage with the folks, just observe as we walk around and be sure that the house is standing, no broken windows, garbage is picked up, etc., etc., etc."

"Sounds like I really want to get over there and meet these people," said Vonny. "What is their ETA?"

"They should be here within the next couple of days. Here are the details that you missed." Colin turned his chair to face Vonny, opened his beer, grabbed a handful of crackers and cheese and carefully began relaying to Vonny the details regarding the Strand's Landing tenants.

"You know Benny is a lawyer. Heck, he works half the summer here using his computer. Anyway, he's met a fellow lawyer who is representing a Latino family that is living 'securely' in Fort Pierce. 'Securely' was Benny's word. They, the family, are in their own private version of the witness protection program. The head of the family, the papas fritis, no that's wrong, that's fried potatoes. Let's try familia primero. Anyway, the father and his family are laying low, keeping a low profile, because in an unnamed South American country, they are personitas non-gratitas. Anyway, that's all you need to know about that piece of the story.

"The grown-up sons of the big persona non-gratitas guy are the ones who will be here for eight to ten weeks. There are two of them. Benny didn't give me any names, sur or otherwise, and they are 'English challenged', again Benny's word choice. The two boys, early twenties, are swimmers who are in training so that they can make a triumphant return to the SA country and reclaim a place in the country's swimming circles, possibly the Olympics, and in the corazones of their amigo countrymen. Honest, that is almost word-for-word what Benny said, not counting the Spanglish, but then I think that he was repeating to me word-for-word what his lawyer friend said to him.

"I think we gotta comply. Benny knows what's up and he said that there'll be no political backlash, no danger, no guerillas on the premises. Live and let live, but spy on them anyway."

"Colin, I must say it again, you are terrible. You're not funny, you know. Cute, but not funny."

Now it was Vonny's turn to pull her chair up real close to Colin's. She put her legs up on Colin's lap then moved one so that a toe or two snuck up at the edge of Colin's frayed, hardly blue, blue jean shorts.

"I may have no sense of humor," said Colin. "But you young lady are shameless. Go to your room. Wait, I'll go with you."

CHAPTER 8

Sunday evening was the usual night that the kids, who were no longer kids, checked in and made Vonny a happy momma. Vonny spoke with each child separately, but was sure to give each child the full story and import of the new, next door tenant; Vonny carefully reviewed the Raymond McGill lineage and then gave a few quick sentences that brought the kids up to date while she worked at not being a gossip or obviously judgmental:

Uncle Ray spent the last almost thirty years in the police force in Baltimore.

- He was injured, shot actually, in the line of duty and is lucky to be alive.
- He was blinded in that incident, had a long recuperation time, went to what he called "blind school" to get "reconditioned" (his term) He uses a collapsible white cane. Might have on sunglasses/not sure about his preferences.
- He's rented next door for the summer (probably about 10 weeks).
- We are all taking the high road and are not going to feel sorry for him, but instead help him in this phase of his life.

Ronny, Jack and Erin were excited to be able to finally meet Uncle Ray. They had heard a lot about him from cousins and aunts and uncles and even their parents: funny stuff, boyhood pranks, explanations of photographs or "family relics" from the distant past. All three siblings promised to be polite and to respect Ray's current status and his privacy.

Vonny thought the calls went well. She had been worried that the kids would ask her (and then when they arrived home, ask Ray) a lot of prying questions, but they each seemed to be satisfied with the information that their mom had given them. Ronny and Dan would be home in five days. Jack and Lindy and Erin and Carrie would be arriving for the 4th of July holiday. Vonny told them to be prepared for a family invasion on the 4th. She was planning to invite most of Ray's siblings and their children, but only those who lived close by. There'd probably be a total of about 35 people counting some O'Briens and a couple of Jacksons.

When Vonny finished her telephone duties, she checked the documents on her computer and printed off her Christmas card list. As the five page, double spaced, list spit out of the printer, she took each page, hand numbered it and then began to peruse the list and circle the family members to invite to reunite with Ray. Vonny and Colin had briefly discussed having a family reunion over the 4th of July weekend. There was only a few days before the 4th, so Vonny stayed right at the computer and created a right-to-the-point invitation that she'd guilt Colin to get into the mail in the morning. She determined to ask everyone to RSVP so that she could inform them about Ray's blindness, she didn't think it PC to mention blindness on the invitation. She had the addresses and the invitation, and it was primarily Colin's family anyway, so he surely wouldn't balk at some easy paperwork in the morning. She returned to the list and put a check mark next to the names of out-of-towners that she'd be sure to send photographs and a note to after the reunion.

"Colin," Vonny shouted. "Come here and let me explain something to you."

No response, not even a "harrumph".

"Colin! You're avoiding me. I'm at the computer. Come on!"

No response, no "coming".

Vonny avoided a third call and went looking for Colin. He was in bed, again looking cute, sound asleep while snuggling his book as though it were a Teddy Bear. She gently removed the book, *Murder at the National Cathedral* by Margaret Truman, kissed Colin on the cheek, turned out his reading lamp and left the room.

HEY...IT'S A PARTY AND A FAMILY REUNION
AT THE O'BRIENS, IN THE SPRINGS, ON JULY 4TH !!!
"SPECIAL GUEST OF HONOR"

RAY MCGILL (THAT'S RIGHT RAYMIE)

FROM BALTIMORE, RETIRED, AND NOW VACATIONING IN MAPLE SPRINGS.

WE WILL PROVIDE ITEMS TO GRILL (VEGGIE AND MEAT) ALONG WITH DRINKS.

BRING "FAMILY FRIENDLY FAVORITE FOOD" TO SHARE.

RONNY, DAN, JACK, LINDY, ERIN AND CARRIE WILL BE HERE TOO

IT'S A MUST TO CALL VONNY TO RSVP, ASAP.

CHAPTER 9

In the morning, when Colin returned from the post office, he parked his car on the lawn to give it a quick wash. It was a new, red, Honda Fit and he assured the guys at his garage that this car was going to last him 200,000 miles. He had said that about his last three cars, but hadn't reached the 200,000 mile mark with any car yet. As he took the bucket and chamois from the Amish shed, he heard voices that he thought were coming from the front porch next door. He was really trying to give Ray his privacy and to not be a nuisance or pry into what Ray was doing, but yet he walked around in the street to the front of his house to see if indeed the voices were coming from Ray's porch.

"Colin, get your buns over here. You shoulda told me that we had company." It was Sheriff Joe Green, the Chautauqua County Sheriff and a friend of Colin's, sitting on Ray's porch.

"What's this 'we' business?" answered Colin as he climbed the stairs to the porch and shook hands and gave Joe one of those awkward man-handshake-pull-in-hug-back-slap-greetings.

"Colin," said Ray. "I let Joe here pick me up and bring me home. I had walked through the Midway Park and when I came out onto Route 430, I got turned around and was disoriented. Don't tell Sally."

"I saw this guy, the white cane was a give-away, that I thought was having an orientation problem, and as the sheriff's code told me to, I stopped to see if I could help, and here we are. He says he knows you."

"We've met," said Colin. Ray laughed.

"I spent the better part of my youth in his company. That explains a lot, doesn't it?" Colin continued.

"I'd say that you're the better man for it," said Sheriff Joe. Ray laughed.

The three men, friends, relatives and mutual friends, talked for a while, each carefully assuring the others of their role in their relationships and in The Springs. Ray made it clear that he was just a visitor, retired and independent. Colin was sure that the other two knew his role around these parts: retired, yearrounder, kind neighbor. And Joe, as his title implied, expressed his concern for the county, its residents and the thousands of visitors who showed up annually. "We got a good thing going 'round here," said Joe. "Any trouble spoiling your stay, you let me know. Okay, Ray?"

"Gotcha," said Ray. "I got Colin right next door so what could go wrong?" Colin laughed.

"You want to tell him or should I?" said Joe to Colin.

"Tell me what?" said Ray.

"You remind me later Ray and I will give you the short version of what's been called the 'situation in Maple Springs' from a couple of years ago," said Colin.

"I gotta get back on the road," said Joe. "We are starting a campaign warning people about fireworks for the upcoming holiday. Last year we had three kids get burned, not severe but scarring nonetheless, and we are determined to not have a repeat of that action. Most of those sparkling and loud fireworks are illegal in New York State, ya know."

Before he left, Joe gave Colin a pile of pamphlets and asked him to distribute them to the families in The Springs, especially the families with children.

"He seems like a nice guy," said Ray after Joe left. "I told him my background and some of the training I had. We have a lot in common. A lot not in common too. He said he had kids and I told him to bring them by for swimming at the community dock. What's he got? Two? Three?"

"Try eight, seven of them boys. Sophia is just walking; she's one. Tone, turning five, was born right in the middle of a murder investigation down here five summers ago. I got appointed as a deputy and we, I'm including the whole sheriff's department, cleared up that situation in about a week. That's 'the situation' that I said I'd tell you about."

"Brian indicated on his 3D map that in the second cottage down, on the right as you head to the lake, on Lakeview that there was a murder in what he labeled as the Stone's Cottage. I was hoping for a report on that event," said Ray.

Colin easily gave Ray a synopsis of "the situation" surrounding the death of Mr. Stone and the murder of Mrs.

Stone. He presented the information matter-of-factly not wanting to rehash all the details and recount all the personalities involved and he did not want to slip into self-promotion when he explained his role in solving the crime. He felt like he was reading a synopsis from a book jacket as he relayed the facts.

After Colin's succinct "situation" explanation, Ray had a couple quick questions and then the two discussed what each had planned for the day.

"Sally will be here after lunch and we will see how much I retained after yesterday's death march around The Springs. Then we are off to Tom's Tavern for pool lessons. I have been playing with both Deanna, at her house, and with Adam at various haunts in Baltimore and I think we can have some fun at Tom's while everyone's here. I was headed to Tom's when Sheriff Joe saved me from the perils of 430. I was just checking out how long it would take me to walk there."

Ray got up and was headed into the house, probably to put on his sneakers, and Colin was quiet, thinking.

"Yes," said Ray turning back to Colin. "I can hang out in bars and avoid 'the bottle'. And yes, I can play pool. Now I have to get guidance from a partner, but when I get my help dog, I will make sure to get one that has pool skills."

Colin sat perfectly still, thinking, then laughing. Ray came out with sneakers in hand just as Sally drove up and parked on the lawn.

"Raymond, you slacker. I said be ready to go at ten and here you are bare footed and it is 10:05. Chop chop, we have hills to climb…'climb every mountain'… and Tom is opening early for us so we need to be there on time. He's offered us a free lunch of his famous chicken wings, hot for me, sissy for you, so let's not snub the man," said Sally all the while bouncing on the balls of her feet in mock stretching.

"Hi Sally. Don't be too hard on Raymondo here. Sheriff Joe and I kept him talking and messed up his getting ready," said Colin.

Sally stopped bouncing. "How'd Joe happen to join you two down here?" asked Sally.

"Gotta go, car to wash, and I have to meet Vonny in town to have a late lunch with her mother," said Colin as he jumped off the porch and headed home. "See you later Ray. We'll talk about the family reunion after supper or so."

Colin could hear Ray sputtering and calling "wait, wait" but he quickly got out of sight, hoping to remain unseen until Ray and Sally had hit the road.

CHAPTER 10

Vonny and Colin drove down Summit into The Springs, just getting home from a very late lunch followed by an unscheduled trip to the local Med Alert Clinic. They saw Ray walking along at a quick pace with his cane leading the way making furious passes left and right insuring that he was on the road and not headed into roadside underbrush.

"Good day Ray," said Vonny sticking her head out of the passenger's window as Colin slowed the car close to Ray and then stopped as Ray did same, "Hope we didn't scare you."

"I heard your car coming down the road. I don't scare easily," said Ray.

"It could have been anyone driving towards you. Some strange Maple Springs' inhabitant," said Vonny.

"No, I can tell your car. Not all cars sound alike you know. You have two cars. This one that you are in is the smaller of the two. That other one sounds like a truck. Is it?"

"No," said Vonny. "It's a Nissan. I usually drive it. It is loud. We left it in town to get inspected and to have an oil change. Maybe it will sound better when I get it back."

"Hope you didn't inspect it on my account, said Ray. "You know too, you could go slower. By the rough sounding engine and the speed as the car passes the house, I am sure it's you. Colin is too prissy to drive fast. He could never catch me when we raced on our bikes back in the day."

"We did not get it inspected for you," said Vonny. "New York State law requires a yearly inspection. Don't you do that in Maryland?"

"Yes, we have annual inspections that are focused mainly on emissions, but I forgot to have my car looked at or I would have driven it up here," said Ray and he didn't wait for Vonny's reaction but continued talking. "I gotta finish this walk before I have my chicken pot pie, thanks to Vicki's TV Dinners. Then I will walk over, Colin says that we have a family reunion to discuss/cancel/postpone/reschedule. Make coffee, black, decafe. I'll be there in twenty-five minutes."

Ray stopped talking, got his cane and himself in motion and was gone before Vonny could rebuff his claim that she drove too fast, inform him that Colin was not prissy or tell him he needn't bother coming for coffee. Instead, she laughed and thought of what she could serve with that coffee when Ray found his way to the bistro set under their carport/pavilion.

CHAPTER 11

A man of his word, Ray was Johnny-on-the-spot in twenty-five minutes. Vonny placed a cup of black coffee in front of each of the three assembled reunion planners and explained to Ray about the contents of the small bowl of cookies in the center of the round table. Ray quickly found his cup and held it carefully by the handle using his left hand.

"Colin calls these chocolate morsels 'Grandma Kitty's Christmas Magic', but we have them all year long," said Vonny referring to the round, chocolate, frosted cookies in the bowl. "I hope they meet with your approval."

Ray placed his right hand directly in front of himself, flat on the surface of the small, round table and slid it carefully, lightly, over the table surface until it came to the bowl. He snagged a cookie and took it close to his face, not to his mouth, but to his nose. Colin and Vonny, unconsciously, simultaneously snagged. Unison sniffing occurred, there was also positive vocalization and then the actual use of language to signify the perfection of the morsels.

"Oh, I haven't had any of Mom's cookies in years," said Ray.

"You haven't lost your touch m' dear. They're great," said Colin.

"Oh, Grandma Kitty, thanks for the recipe and the lessons," said Vonny.

A second course of cookies in a separate identical bowl that Vonny had sequestered on the seat of the fourth chair of the bistro set was enjoyed and then the hastily convened reunion committee was set to commence its work. This second cookie was "Grandma Kitty's Peanut Butter Pattie".

Vonny said that she thought that a discussion of local housekeeping rules regarding the arrival of Springers and catch-up on the arrival of Ronny and Dan and Deanna, Adam, Kenzie and Tori would surely have to take precedent.

"First things first," said Colin.

"Ok, but it's my first thing first and your first thing will be second," said Ray. "What's the story on the Med Alert Clinic that you skimmed over earlier? Why'd you stop there? Who got treated for what?"

"It was nothing," said Vonny. "I had an allergic reaction to something that I came in contact with at lunch. I got an immediate rash, thought my throat was going to close, breathing was restricted, but a quick shot of a Benadryl-like med and I was fine. Colin, my cute little Doctor on call, got me right to the clinic and I was fine. It was me, not the food. The owner of the restaurant showed up at the clinic, with my purse and my mother who we had left at the restaurant, and both ladies were very nervous. I have to go back to the restaurant tomorrow and we are going to make a list of ingredients and go from there to see what might have caused the reaction so that I can avoid that ingredient and get tested for like items. No need to be of concern."

"There! My turn," said Colin. "We'll keep you posted Ray. Moving along. My first input, now a first that is really a second, is to invite you to the 'Summer Wine Festival' that will take place on Wednesday evening at the Stone cottage, now called 'The Maple Springs Cottage'. The Cottage is part of the Maple Springs Inn's sprawl here in The Springs. The Festival is a tradition started years ago by the Stone family. The get-together starts the social season down here in this 'beauty spot on Lake Chautauqua.'"

"I know about this kick-off. Brian told me although he said he never got to go because it happened before his family got here for the summer. It's all falling into place now: the 'situation', the Stone Cottage, Deputy O'Brien, Joe Green. Will I be safe? Should I come packin'? You know, concealed carry. Will there be enough people here to make it worth having?" asked Ray.

Vonny leaned forward and put a hand on Colin's arm to silence him and she jumped in to answer Ray's questions and to hopefully then get the conversation turned in the direction of the family reunion that was to take place in less than two weeks.

"Yes," said Vonny. "The Festival has been earlier these last few years because William and Elizabeth from the Inn now own the cottage and they have the place rented for most of the summer. We have to enjoy the Festival when- ever the cottage is available to us. Just join us there, meet some folks and enjoy some great food. Okay?

"Now, my first is third and we have to get to the re-union. Humor me, pretend you care, tell me that you think it is important and that you'll help," concluded Vonny

Colin and Ray humored Vonny and within the next half hour the McGill/O'Brien/Jackson Family Reunion, the first in quite some time, was planned. Vonny read the invitation list aloud and no one was added, and because Colin had already mailed the invitations, no one was deleted from the guest list.

"A family reunion is a reunion of the whole family, not part of the family. Let's leave things as they are. Even the uninvited are invited. What's another hot dog and a scoop of potato salad? The reunion will take on a life of its own. So be it," said Colin formalizing and finalizing the commit-tee meeting.

Vonny offered more cookies and more coffee and then excused herself to make some work related telephone calls to family members of "her residents".

"You're a lucky man, Colin," said Ray when he knew that Vonny was inside the house. "I knew she was a sweetheart back in the Freddie days. I'd say that she's the brains behind this outfit."

"No argument from me on that point," responded Colin.

Just then loud music, Latin music, filled the air. Colin startled, but not so with Ray.

"Yikes, that's loud. Didn't that startle you," asked Colin.

"Nah, I heard it on a lower volume and then it got turned up. It was pretty loud earlier today too. You and Vonny were in town when it was blaring. I think folks were moving into a cottage across the street, down one house, Strand's I think. The truck they had was noisy, the delivery guys were loud, and foul, and the guys that stayed after everything was unloaded were loud too. Loud in Spanish. There was a lot of Spanglish too. Bunch of guys, I'd say," said Ray.

"Oh yea, I shoulda told you about that crew. Ben Strand called and said that there would be some young guys there for a few weeks. Young guys, swimmers, looking for anonymity. Ben said just two guys. Just like Brian, Ben can't get here for most of the summer, daughter is getting married, so others have rented the house. They'll settle down or someone will have to mention the loudness of the musica Espanol."

"Colin, you habla Uds espanole?" asked Ray.

"No, not even un piquito," replied Colin.

"I got all that down," said Ray. "Baltimore has a large Latino community. Well it's not so much that it is large, but it is active; Spanish festivals, lots of restaurantes, two or three Hispanics on the city council, and I am sorry to say, but there are a few bad hombres too. Lots of Hispanics on the police force, even two or three ladies. Those guys, and ladies, were tougher on their youth than us white guys were. And the youth listen to them too. There's a lot to be said for the way the Hispanic families teach respect, especially respect for elders and even for the authorities. I had several Hispanic partners and one time when I was sent back to the street after what I would call, to use your word, a 'situation', I was part of outreach in a storefront youth center. My Spanish got real good, bueno, real fast. We'll give our hermanos a couple days to settle down and then I can talk to them. I was beat after Sally left, but when the newcomers arrived and were so loud, I hit the road for a bit. That's what I was doing when you stopped to talk when you were coming home. I bet the gang went grocery shopping, but are now home for the evening."

"Right. We will give them some settling in time and then someone, not me, will have a friendly talk with them. I got Ben's instructions," said Colin and then he proceeded to fill in Ray with the particulars of the scenario that Ben Strand had provided. "Guess we have to give them their space," concluded Colin.

Ray confessed that he was itching to walk again and asked Colin to join him. Ray explained that his walking in Baltimore was a lot slower and a lot more dangerous and he was enjoying the fresh air, the feel of the sun and the bird songs.

"Bird songs? What'd ya mean?" asked Colin.

"Colin, it's like we're back in Webelos and I have to help you with your birding badge. Remember, we had to be able to identify ten birds by sight and a different ten birds by their song. We cheated, but we got that damn badge and that was all we wanted anyway. Since those Cub Scout days, I have always been interested in birds. You'd be surprised how many different birds live in a city. I don't know why, but they do live there. One time, Brenda and I had an apartment on a top floor, the eighth, and there was a balcony. If I could have sub-leased to birds, I could have made a fortune. Right after we moved in, we went away on a long weekend, gambling at sea I think, and when we came home, there were several nests out there. Eggs too. How do ya send soon-to-be-mommies out into the cold world. Well, you know the story: we fed them, they stayed, they left, they returned, they crapped. You could say that we had a bird's eye view of the birds. We never used that balcony. It was too small and already occupied. When we moved, the building had gone condo by then, we made sure the new folks liked birds. Actually, I think it was the birds that helped us to sell the place. Anyway, to make a long story short, I have continued my lust for birds to this day. Since what I cavalierly call 'my accident', it's their song styling that captures me. It's not tweeting, it's styling. Deanna gave me a clock that broadcasts each hour-on-the-hour and each sound is a different bird song. Two o'clock is a robin, midnight is the blue jay and so forth. I was sitting on my porch, Brian's porch, and just listening and I sorted out eight different bird songs. Bet there's even more species living in these parts."

"Ray, you are something. I'm not sure what. I see birds,

but I can't say that I have actually hear them. I've been here for five years. How pathetic is that?"

"Pathetic. I agree. We'll have to do something about that deficiency in your awareness profile. Either that or I will have to strip you of that Webelos badge."

"Tomorrow. We will start tomorrow. Unless you have plans," said Colin.

"I do have a full dance card, but will fit you in. Meanwhile shall we walk, or we could salsa right here in your carport. The music is still playing."

"Walking it is. You sure it's okay? Got your cane? Tell me when you're winded. Tell me to shut up."

And they were off down Whiteside Parkway, a quick left turn onto Lakeview Avenue and then along the lake with the sun busy creating a splendid sunset that Colin remarked on and Ray somehow enjoyed.

CHAPTER 12

Colin woke up to the sound of car doors closing. It sounded like the doors were attached to a vehicle in Ray's driveway.

He rolled over and looked at the clock; 8:36.

He non-gracefully got out of bed and stood before the drawn bedroom curtains. It was none of his business who deigned to pull a car into that driveway. Colin wasn't in charge of Ray. Ray wasn't poor Ray. Forget it.

By the time he got through berating himself, when he quickly pulled the curtains aside, almost taking them off the inset spring curtain rod at the top of the window casement, he failed to have the car in view. Perhaps it was going in front of his house. He hurried to the front porch. Damn, they went the other way.

"It's none of my business," Colin said out loud. "I shoulda moved quicker."

"Hi Colin. Lookin' good." It was Eileen Miller, in her truck, and she let out a wolf whistle without even using her fingers and then she drove quickly down the street. It looked like she was headed to the Maple Springs Cottage. She was probably going to help set up for the Summer Wine Festival.

Colin then realized that he was on the porch, by the street, for anyone passing by to see. He was wearing his

summer, tie-dyed, tattered, too short, too tight pajamas.
He quickly got back inside and calmed himself with khaki
shorts and an XXL t-shirt. Oh, and coffee. A note on the
Keurig told him that Vonny had gone to *Tres Hermanas*
to check on the cause of her scary, allergic reaction from
yesterday. Colin and Vonny had pretty much determined
to not broadcast the particulars of Vonny's reaction and to
definitely not mention the name of the restaurant. They did
not want to have people think that Vonny had experienced
food poisoning or that there was a cleanliness problem at
the restaurant. They did not want to have people avoiding
Tres Hermanas which was one of their favorite restaurants.
Vonny was meeting early with one of the owners, Grace that
had come to the clinic, and the two of them were going to
list all of the ingredients of the dishes that Vonny and Colin
had shared for lunch. The practice of sharing dishes was
one of the reasons that Colin and Vonny liked *Tres Hermanas*. The fact that they had shared dishes meant that it
was something that bothered only Vonny. It wasn't bad food
or unsanitary conditions. Colin was confident that Vonny
would get this situation solved. Her note said too that she
would go right to work and would not be home for supper.
It was "sip and paint night" and she would be home at about
nine o'clock. "Love ya", "you're the best" and "XOXOXO"
completed the note.

Colin then realized that he had twelve hours to himself.
There were lots of "get-ready-for-summer" things to do so

he put on sturdy sneakers and was ready to get to work. He thought that first he should see if Ray was around. Colin knew that Sally wasn't going to be in The Springs today. Ray had mentioned that last night, but then too maybe there was a change of plans and it was her car he heard earlier. Sally still could have come to take Ray somewhere. Ray knew no one else in The Springs. It might have been Sheriff Joe Green. Ray had met him. Out of concern for Ray, Colin walked over to the fence and called for him by name, loudly.

"Hey Ray! Come on out and play. You in there?"

Colin stood at the fence, noticed the backdoor was closed, saw or heard no sign of movement. There was no response.

One last, loud call and Colin left the fence and got to work emptying the carport of the summer, outdoor furniture. Then he swept the cement and got out his pressure washer and cleaned that floor so that it looked like it hadn't just spent the last 6 months under inches, and at times feet, of snow. He wanted it washed and dried so he could put down the new rattan rugs that he had ordered on line. The rugs were in his neighbor's garage waiting for just the right moment to be put in place to surprise Vonny. She'd seen the rugs on the L.L. Bean web site, but passed them up because they were too expensive. Colin, one night in February after Vonny went to bed, found very similar rugs (maroon and brown chevron patterned) on a discount home furnishing site, HOMZZZ.com. He ordered them from the sale items section. He received a 25% discount for new customers and free delivery if the order was over one hundred dollars. It took the rugs three weeks to get there, but he didn't need them in March anyway. Today was installation-day and make-Vonny-happy-day all rolled into one.

While the carport was drying, Colin created three hanging baskets that he had planned for when he first saw a picture of the final product in a gardening magazine at the end of last summer. The basket promised to grow huge quickly with colorful, in this case white and purple verbena and bacopa, standing tall. Creeping jenny and banana fern would insure that the pot would look full. There'd be no common geraniums or petunias in these three glamorous baskets that would hang from wrought iron plant hangers on the edge of the summer pavilion. In the winter the pavilion was a handy-dandy car port, but come summer, it became a pavilion and housed furniture, people and good times. This year there would also be three gorgeous hanging planters.

The morning went by quickly, but Colin accomplished a lot of things on his "get-ready-for-summer" list of things to do. Usually by this date, most item on Colin's list had been crossed off and he had only to enjoy the summer. This year he didn't even get to the list in May, as he usually did, because he and Vonny had spent most of May working on a fixer-upper with Jack and Lindy in Vermont. Some construction professionals and Vermont friends were also part of the work crew. It had been hard work, but a lot of fun

too because they worked all day and then slept in a tent at
night. Thank goodness the bathroom was intact or that tent
living might have been unbearable. The Vermont house
was pretty much in the post-fixer-upper state and now
Colin was home to get ready for summer; he was ready to
attack that list.

Colin took a break to make a quick lunch, realizing
that he had neglected to have breakfast. He sat on the front
porch and ate his vanilla yogurt that he had liberally laced
with Cherrios and chocolate chips. He also had half of a
bagel with peanut butter and a bottle of spring water that
he had bought from some Amish boys that had been selling
their product door to door. The boys, probably nine or ten,
Jacob and Levi, had guaranteed that their water was from a
spring back in the woods on their property and that it was
perfectly natural and pure. They called it 'Yoder Water'.
The Yoder boys had a small cart pulled by a small horse and
they made the rounds of the small enclaves along the lake,
with a hand bell sounding their arrival. They were cute
little boys and they seemed to be having success with their
venture. "Amish child entrepreneurs" was a new concept
for Colin. He was sure that their cart would soon contain
home baked goods, home grown vegetables and a knitted
item or two before the end of their second full week of sales.

Just as he finished his tasty lunch, the telephone rang
and he hurried inside with dishes in hand and grabbed the
phone. It was Vonny calling.

"Hi Hon. I am in the parking lot at work, but thought that I should call you. I got time. Grace, uno of the tres sisters, was all ready for me when I got there. She had the recipes and even the spice containers. We narrowed the culprit down to the salsa on the bean quesadillas or the diced tomatoes that she had on the side for us to sprinkle on the refried beans. I think we both had both of those items?"

"Hello my sweet," answered Colin. "I was wondering if I would hear from you. I'm fine. I slept well and you'll be glad to know that I had no digestive tract reactions. I was worried about a delayed reaction even though yours was pretty immediate. I'm fine," said Colin and he paused waiting for a reaction from Vonny: a laugh, an apology, anything.

"I'm glad to hear that you are fine. Now back to me. Grace is checking with her tomato source to see if there was a spray used on the vines or if there was some sort of crop wash that might have bothered me. No one else, no other customers or staff had a problem. I am going to let her work it out. She'll get to us ASAP. But on to the big news of the day or let's call it the mystery of the day really. Ready?"

"What are you going on about?" asked Colin.

"Well, I was sitting in the restaurant's office. It looks out onto the parking lot on Center Street. I saw Ray, I am sure it was him, walking with a man in a black suit. Ray had his cane, I am sure it was him, but I didn't know who his companion was. But, I did figure it out. Want a clue?" Vonny didn't wait for Colin to answer. This was her telephone demeanor, lots of talk, questions and moving from one topic to another with absolutely no transitions or warning.

"There was a stretch white limo in the parking lot." Vonny let that fact lay there. Colin did not take the bait. He'd wait her out.

"The twosome was going in the doors of the Center Street Counseling Center. You know that the CSCC is right next door to Tres Hermanas. What's that about?"

This time, Colin failed to wait her out.

"Bill Morris! Musta been!" said Colin. "White limo. Ray knows him. I heard a car. Bill always wears a dark suit. Perhaps a stop at CSCC and then a fare of some kind. Stop for what? What else do ya know? Come on."

"Can't stand it, can you?" said Vonny. "Well, I looked at my watch, it was 9:55. They were in there for an hour. Yes, I waited. When Grace and I finished talking, I waited in the car and saw them come out of the building and get into the limo and off they went. I would have followed them, but I had to get to work. Stopped for wine for the 'sip' part of this evening's activity and now I have to get inside and look productive for a bit. What d' ya think that was about?"

Vonny did not wait for an answer to her last question. That too was part of her unique telephone etiquette. "Bye, love ya."

Colin couldn't stand it. He got out the Jamestown telephone directory and turned to the Community Services pages. There it was, Center Street Counseling Center, CSCC. Almost half of that page consisted of a list of the services offered at the premier, county counseling center. Colin did not have to go down the list very far. AA was the first entry and it even listed the days and times of the meetings. Bingo. That was it. Ray didn't mention meetings although he was up front about a problem, "the bottle", but he had no questions for Colin about local AA offerings. It was great that Bill took him. Colin would have taken him if asked. Why didn't Bill leave Ray and just pick him up an hour later. It can be a real chore to sit through a meeting any meeting as an outsider. Bill's a great guy.

A knock on the door snapped Colin into the here and now.

"Hey Neph, wanna go shoot some pool? Remember, Deanna and the rest of my gang, and your gang too, will be along in a couple days and I want to look cool when I run the table wearing shades at Tom's over the weekend. Do you think it's okay for the girls, age 16, to go in there? How late does Tom's stay open? Do they have air?"

"Enough. Holy shamoly, Ray. You just asked about 20 questions. You used to do that as a kid and it drove me crazy. I hoped you'd be done with that, but then I bet it was probably a good interrogation tactic in B-more," said Colin. "Anyway, yes. Yes. 2:00 am. Yes. Let's go."

Colin and Ray spent the early afternoon at Tom's. They played pool, with Colin sitting back from the table and giving minimal instructions mostly having to do with moving left or moving right. Ray had been there twice with Sally, so he had the ambiance down and as Ray said, "A pool table is a pool table is a pool table. I saw a lot of them when I was impaired with the facility of sight. My game has improved greatly since my 'situation'. It's like this cue is a ghost limb that I'm automatically operating."

Colin and Ray were home relaxing on Ray's porch by mid-afternoon. They had had to share Tom's with The Happy Hookers. The Hookers were a group of knitting ladies who met at Tom's on Wednesdays for lunch, knitting and a drink or two. Tom opened the kitchen early to accommodate the Hookers. Their knitted items went to "the boys" in the middle-east. Tom had been one of "the boys" and he was glad to accommodate the ladies.

As they sat on Ray's porch talking, Colin purposely never brought up the fact that Vonny had seen Ray and Bill Morris in town. Colin didn't pry, didn't even subtly hint that Vonny was in town or that he had called Ray across the fence earlier, but hadn't raised him. He's an adult, thought Colin. He can and should have his own schedule, friends and goals. I'll ask him later Colin thought. Probably ask point blank, we're related, it's okay.

"Hang on, Colin," said Ray. "They're cranking up the musica. Looks like our solitude is in jeopardy."

Ray was right. Music, which obviously had South America origins, sounded loud and clear. Lots of drums, voices and rhythm instruments filled the air.

"Told ya," said Ray. "I heard it revving. Guess los muchachos must be home. What's our time frame for a father-to-son talk happening on their porch?"

Just then Colin saw someone walking briskly down the street, cutting across an adjoining lawn, seemingly headed for Strand's Landing. At first Colin wasn't sure who was under the big straw hat, but he soon recognized the large purse that was clutched under her right arm. Although he could not see Elgin, the pursedog, Colin was sure that the dog was along for the ride in that purse. He was sure too that the brisk walker was Binky King. Binky was a longtime summer resident and third generation homeowner. Vonny and Binky had become friends over the past few years. Colin and Binky, and Elgin, had shared the adventure of finding Selma Stone's body four years earlier when there was a "situation" in The Springs. Hard as it might be to believe, at one point during that adventure Elgin had endured Colin holding him. In fact, one day weeks later when Binky and hubby Bernie had to take a quick run to the emergency room at the Westfield Hospital, something to do with an embedded fish hook, Elgin had spent several hours at the O'Brien cottage. That brief piece of respite care had been a first for Elgin. He was not in the least scarred because of the experience, but Binky suffered the pangs of desertion and having been an unfit mother. That respite experience has not since been repeated.

Colin explained to Ray that a neighbor lady was headed up the Strand's steps. "Lured by the music no doubt." The music stopped. It didn't get lowered, it stopped, and talking, not shouting, could be heard.

"Get ready, Colin. The music's revving."

Colin and Ray sat quietly, still on the porch. The rev of music settled at an acceptable sound level. It could just barely be heard, base mostly. Voices could also be heard.

Soon Binky exited the Strand's cottage, gracefully moved down the steps and was soon in the road. She headed down Forest Lawn Avenue and right to the bottom step of Ray's porch.

"Colin, love, are you lost? Your porch is next door. Who is this adorable man? No invite to sit? I'd love a summer beer. The one that needs orange or the one that calls for lemon or is it lime? No glass, love that bottle."

By the time she finished guilting Colin and Ray into offering her a beer, Binky, and Elgin of course, were up the stairs and planted into the only wicker on the porch. It was a rocker.

"Well, Colin?" Colin took the obvious hint and introduced Binky to his uncle and his uncle to Binky.

"If you're here for the summer, you won't be playing music at that volume I hope," said Binky pointing to the cottage across the street.

Ray explained that he was there for the summer, but that he was an earbuds man and he'd be quiet as a mouse.

"My music is the slower, softer, old fogey music. I keep my music preferences to myself. That way people judge me on my sparking personality and not my taste in music. I don't share my books for that same reason, and another couple of reasons also."

Binky reminded Colin about her drink preference and he left quickly for home and returned to gales of laughter carrying two Blue Moon beers with orange slices carefully topping the bottles and a lemon-lime sparkling soda for Ray.

"Colin, you're wicked. This charming man actually is your uncle. I thought you were being clever or trying to be clever. He freely admitted that he was related to you. He actually told me that you and he were raised by wolves. I like this man. He's delightful."

"Binky, you have just called Ray here adorable, charming and delightful and I can't even get a clever," said Colin.

They all laughed and had a sip and fell into easy talk about The Springs, Ray's summer plans, the Summer Wine Festival and then the music situation at Strand's Landing.

"I could hear them at my house, down the street toward the lake, the Promanade, and over two or three cottages by Lakeview Avenue. Too loud, I told them. They were very much taken aback, but they listened. They too are adorable and I think they will be more simpatico as the days pass. I invited them to the Summer Wine Festival, they declined, might not drink, and to my porch anytime they'd like. Bernie will enjoy them. He speaks espanol. We have lots of Hispanics working for us in California. They are hard workers, very creative and treat each other and us with respect. Sorry, it looks like I painted them all with the same brush, but it was a positive brush so don't think me racist. Carmentia, the lady who cooks for us is heaven. I want to bring her here, maybe next year, but she has grandchicos and chicas to help take care of.

"So, the music will be softer. Let me know if it gets too loud. I suppose we should give them their space. They speak loudly too. When I pounded on the door, it sounded like there was 4 or 5 people in there, but I saw only two, brothers for sure."

"Ben Strand told me there would only be two young men. They are South Americans who will be swimming in the lake a lot." Colin told Binky this much and then Ray gave a few more details. The three agreed that the visitors could be refreshing and possibly offer some excitement to the summer.

"Bet we don't see much of them. They'll be in the lake or off to Bemus for the nightlife," said Binky. "Oh my, gotta go. I told Bernie I'd be right back. I am making guacamole for tomorrow, going to Steve's for avocados. I am using Carmentia's authentic recipe. Bye, you two adorable men. Happy Colin?" said Binky and the two of them were up, down the stairs and headed home before the other two could even stand and show her what good manners these adorable senior citizens possessed.

"She's a character," said Ray after he knew that Binky was out of ear shot.

"Can you tell me anything about her from her voice, where she's from, age, anything?" Colin blurted out. "I heard that one's other senses inflate, you know increase, when they lose one sense. What I mean is, are your ears and nose working overtime?"

"Colin, it's a good thing Vonny isn't here to hear that non-PC question. Sorry to disappoint yet again, but no, I don't have extrasensory powers these days. I do smell lilacs. Is there a bush nearby? And there was another smell too. I want to say dog. She have dogs at home? Sometimes you carry their smell. All my friends at the center at home with dogs have a whiff of doggie. I can't wait till I do."

"Not only is Binky wearing an essence in abundance, always does, the lilac. She is carrying the dog, essence and all, in her purse, Elgin. Elgin is the name of the dog, not the name of her purse. I am surprised that she didn't introduce you two."

Colin and Ray talked for a while longer and then Ray opted for a nap and Colin went to finish the set-up of the pavilion. He carefully watered the new hanging pots and did some adjusting of plant positions. He then stood back to take in their current incarnation which foretold of an upcoming summer-long-lasting beauty. He then borrowed Dianne Warren's golf cart to fetch the new rugs. Dianne was home in Beaver, PA and had told Colin to use the cart whenever he needed it. The rugs were exactly what Vonny wanted, what Colin could afford and what looked best in the pavilion. Colin then replaced the furniture, rearranging it to go with the placement of the rugs. Vonny could always change the furniture placement later if she wanted to, but for now it looked great and she'd truly love the surprise. She was a sucker for a good surprise. Colin was sure that there would be tears.

Colin returned the golf cart to Dianne's garage, put away the power washer and plumped the throw pillows the way that David Bromstad does during his appearances on all those HGTV shows. Colin then placed small pots of primrose on the two side tables and a vase of forsythia that he'd borrowed from Dianne in the middle of the round picnic table. He'd bring out a few candles later and be all mellow when Vonny appeared with the lovely original painting that she and twenty-five other people were magically, simultaneously, creating this evening.

Colin took a quick shower and read a few of the essays in a book by Brian Doyle. He enjoyed a toasted cheese sandwich made with three cheeses and a slice of tomato on marbled bread. He also had a bowl of his favorite cole slaw and a Switchback beer. All this lead Colin to be relaxed, though he was beat, and anxious for Vonny's return.

"Colin, honey. Wake up. I'm home. Colin."

Colin opened his eyes, but didn't get a chance to talk because Vonny planted a big kiss on his lips and then proceeded to flounce, yes she was flouncing, around the pavilion. She moved from chair to chair enjoying the look and feel of the place where she would surely spend many summer hours.

"Oh Colin! It's all so wonderful; brown and maroon, I thought you hated that. Hanging planters? You said 'no, they are a pain to water'. Oh Colin. I love you. What, no candles, no wine?"

But there were candles. There was wine. Vonny knew there would be. And oh yes, there were tears. Colin knew there would be.

CHAPTER 13

The day of the Summer Wine Festival, held exclusively for Maple Springers, was always a hectic time. In the past, this opening event of the Maple Springs' summer season, was held early in the summer when the Stone family first arrived in The Springs. Both G.E.M. and Selma Stone, and the first Mrs. Stone, Lula, had passed on, but their spirits survived in Maple Springs because of the Festival and because of the lovely community dock that they had bequeathed to the community. Their cottage was now called The Maple Springs Cottage, part of the Maple Springs Inn which was just a short walk up Whiteside Parkway. The Festival was held on the back deck of the Cottage. The Inn rented the Cottage to vacationers and so the Festival date changed according to availability.

William and Elizabeth, Inn proprietors, now sponsored the Festival and were sure to have local wines and beers for sampling. Wineries and breweries gladly gave samples, anything to invite new customers. These libation producers hoped that The Springers would return home to Cleveland, Pittsburgh, etc. and would ask their local purveyors to stock the fine WNY wines and beers. Each attending Springer was to bring an appetizer to share. It was a great evening of catching up, initial meetings and the joy of knowing that The Springs was coming alive, full of summertime promises and surprises.

During the day Colin helped William to move furniture, some even off the large deck onto the thick, bright green lawn, to maximize the flow on the deck. They loaded coolers from the ice machine at the Inn and put down the two electric awnings that were made of canvas and sported a huge print design in colors associated with Mexico. Elizabeth had made huge flowers out of tissue paper that matched the colors of the awnings and the colors of the back side of the house. Originally the house was all pink and white, but the back deck had been reconfigured and decorated by G.E.M. and Selma to remind them of a vacation that they had taken south of the border. The tissue paper flowers, in huge bunches, were in tall containers that looked like the ones found in cemeteries. The awnings, the simple flowers and the orange and yellow cushions on the chairs and small couches proved to be plenty of color to satisfy the eye. The wine, beer and appetizers would satisfy the appetite. The attendees offered each other solace from the road trip that brought them to Maple Springs. Most were tired from a busy winter in wherever and eager for the R & R & R ...Rest and Relaxation and Recreation...that was available in The Springs for the taking.

During the day Colin kept an eye out for returnees. He helped some to unload a car, or an SUV and he even unhitch boats. Most returnees arranged for someone to open their cottage and to give it a good cleaning. It was usually

Eileen Miller who organized a small group of co-workers
who appreciated the seasonal work and who were grateful
for the under-the-table dollars that came their way. The
returnees, to a man or woman, said that they hurried to be
in The Springs for the Festival and they had lots of time to
settle, starting tomorrow. While waiting for the Festival to
start, some sat on their porch, some went to check to see if
their dock had been put in its proper place on the shore and
some were off to Steve's Store, or even off to Wegman's Super
Market, to get a few essentials.

Vonny worked her Wednesday half-day in the morning
and was planning to be home to make her signature appetizer, spinach balls, to take to share at the Festival. She often
took spinach balls to share. She got the recipe from a friend
and tried it out on the kids when they were young. In fact,
Jackson was in nursery school at the time. Jack declared
that these spinach balls were his favoritest food of all time.
When it was his turn to take a treat to school, of course he
had to take those tasty green balls of spinach, cheese and
breadcrumbs. The pre-schoolers en masse hated Jack's
favoritest food of all time. But that did not phase Jack; "All
the more for me," he said.

Once when Colin checked earlier in the day, he saw
Ray on his porch with his laptop. He had on earphones, he
called them 'earbuds', and he seemed like any ordinary vaca-
tioner soaking in some sun, fresh air and calm. Later when
Colin checked, the porch was empty. Colin, sometimes

one to be a worry-wart, was concerned that Ray might have become disoriented again and was wandering on Route 430 hoping Sheriff Green would chance by once more. Colin decided that if after a quick shower and an even quicker lunch that if Ray was not around that he would call him on his cell phone. Maybe he's out walking with Sally, thought Colin. Can't be, he countered his own thoughts, Sally's Honda is nowhere in sight.

"Hello Ray," said Colin into his kitchen telephone, before the shower or lunch. "I'm looking for you. Don't want you lost, or in a ditch somewhere, or to miss the Summer Wine Festival tonight. Call me. You have the number. Bye."

When Colin got out of the shower, the number 2 was flashing on his answering machine:

"Hi honey. Trapped with a family member at work. Thaw the spinach. Love you, miss you, see you soon."

"Hi Colin. I'm talking pooches with Tim and Cindy, on their porch. Join us. We had a pizza from Coppola's. There's crusts left if you are so inclined. You always liked the crust. I pulled off the cheese, left the dough, and you only wanted the crust. We were so cute. Bye."

Colin thawed, dressed and hurried to the McMillan's

and mostly listened as they talked about breeds, temperament, care fundamentals, etc. that had to be considered when taking on a help dog. Ray wasn't fond of the term "seeing eye dog". Tim, retired vet, and Cindy, animal and Tim lover, both had experiences training dogs and in raising dogs to be "suited for service". "Suited for service" was Tim's way of describing the great canines that became partners with a human and made everyone's life easier. Ray was "a-ways-out" from having a help dog, but he needed to be sure of the ramifications of forming that partnership before he jumped into that life style. Perhaps his experiences with the ABC wives had an impact on his reluctance. His friends with help dogs in Baltimore had great experiences, loved their buddies, but there were only eight or ten to talk with. Ray, always a thorough investigator, was content to be in the information-seeking mode for a bit longer. He knew that his facility with the cane had to be top-notch and he wanted to be highly capable with that skinny, white and red friend before he took on a furry friend.

Talk continued regarding dogs, Tim's recent retirement, the upcoming Festival and Ray's summer plans. For Ray, summer would surely be filled with R & R & R, lots of exercise, pool, Deanna, music, reuniting with whatever family members were willing to forgive and forget and accept. Ray also looked forward to reuniting with nature and getting to know some Springers. Tim was eager to take Ray fishing. Cindy offered to help Ray with cleaning supplies and the

Amish girl, Amanda, on her first day on the job at Rays.

By three o'clock, the McMillan porch was empty. They all left intent on getting ready for the Festival. When Ray mentioned that he had no food to share, he was assured that there would be plenty, don't worry. He said he'd bring his guitar and could "play quietly in a corner somewhere". He also said that he had told Tom that he'd play at his Tavern some evening, so he best get some practicing accomplished. When Colin got home, Vonny was there, grateful for the thawed spinach, and she was rolling those delicious orbs so that they could stand in the refrigerator before being baked. Once baked, they'd be placed in a small crock pot and taken to the Festival, devoured and enjoyed.

Things buzzed along at the O'Briens, Ray could be heard tuning, Festival readiness was assured. The Springs in general and the Festival in particular were buzzing with homecomings and renewal. And Vonny, she was glad for the continued civility of The Springs and the Springers as she realized when she walked in her door at 7:30, home from the Festival, that the day was finally over; "It seemed like this day would never end."

"I don't think I sat for more than a half of an hour today, at McMillan's. I too exude a being-pooped attitude," said Colin with a laugh and a dramatic gesture. He loved his own sense of humor.

"It was great to see everyone, not as many as at last year's Festival. It's easy to see why William and Elizabeth are so successful as innkeepers," said Colin. "They didn't exude my storied pooped attitude. They enjoy and really are working without displaying all the effort that we know it takes to make an event 'happen'. Ray was a riot. I am surprised that he can really play that guitar, but the singing is like all the members of our extended family. We even avoid singing Christmas carols, it's that bad. Ray's sure to have a house full of Springers when he has his gig at Tom's."

"My favorite part of the evening," said Vonny, "was when Binky came to the realization that Ray was blind. She met him on his porch. What was she thinking? Was she sitting with the sun in her eyes? Anyway, I loved it too when she offered up Elgin to be Ray's service dog. Right, Elgin would require a service dog and still that could never work. I just thought it was a riot and soooo Binky. Ray was gracious. I think he and Binky are to be summer friends. I also saw Ray was in a quiet conversation with Elizabeth. I bet he, or he and Deanna, spend some time at the Inn. Tim and Cindy are cool with Ray too."

"I think Ray is going to have, exactly, the summer vacation that he has envisioned. Rather than worrying about him bothering us, I think we might have a tough time finding him, or even getting our name onto his already full dance card," said Colin. "I'm going to check the answering machine and close up. Be right to bed."

Vonny "got prone", her cure for all fatigue and confusion. Colin made his brief close-up-the-house tour, saw that there were no phone messages and by the time he returned to the bedroom, Vonny had ended the day that she thought would never end. Ah sleep, one of nature's cure-alls. Colin made an effort to read, his steady reading habit had taken a hit. Soon he was ignoring Margaret Truman and had joined Vonny in that proness and sleep combination.

CHAPTER 14

Colin awoke to the sound of pan rattling in the kitchen. His *My Pillow* over his head did not prove muffle-worthy. He, just to be funny, put on his Alfred E. Newman t-shirt and staggered into the kitchen. Vonny, wise woman that she was, ignored him. That ignoring did not squelch Colin's attempts to be entertaining. Moaning and snuggling her from behind forced Vonny to turn around, weapon in hand, to threaten him with her wooden spoon.

"You are not funny," said Vonny trying to stifle her smile. She proved to be Harvey Kormanesque and broke out laughing in Colin's arms, the spoon no longer brandished.

"Seriously, you ninny, I have to get these pies in the oven or they will never be done for supper. I checked the answering machine and now we know that Dan and Ronny will be here early. I also saw Ray when I went out to get the *Post-Journal*. He was headed out for a walk, and he said that his company, all four, will be here early too. Ray and I decided on dinner here for all nine of us. He's grilling. Yes, it's safe, he's had lots of lessons. I am making a big salad and grape pies. Don't speak. He's grilling meat for the carnivores and vegetable shish kebabs for the civilized among us. You are to head to Steve's for a couple loaves of that great

Amish rye bread that he sells. It should be fresh today. He only sells it on weekends. Now you may speak."

Colin returned to the bedroom, dressed, attended to his sanitary needs and rejoined Vonny in the kitchen.

"I hope those pies are either sweet potato or Concord grape or else I will return with an Amish apple pie," said Colin with arms folded in a mock pout.

"It's grape today, I just told you that, and it'll be sweet potato for July 4th," said Vonny. "I have the pie filling made. Remember I prepared all those Concords at the end of last summer. I froze 5 1/3 cups of pulp in a zip-lock bag, so each bag, I got three, is a pie. I am working on the crusts. I made the dough yesterday when the spinach balls were resting in the fridge. Now I have to roll the dough out and assemble the pies. Piece of cake, or in this case piece of pie."

Colin laughed at her play on words. Vonny had a great sense of humor even if Colin thought that she didn't always appreciate his keen, often topical and political, grasp and/or demonstration of the truly humorous.

"Love ya. Kiss, kiss," and Colin was off to Steve's. Yes, the bread was in and it was incredibly fresh. No need to get a pie. Colin did not buy beer because he knew Dan and Ronny didn't drink, Ray had his reasons for abstaining and Colin guessed that Deanna and Adam respected Ray's situation. There was some wine at home somewhere and a few beer in the fridge. He'd make his lemonade and ice tea combination. They also had seltzer water and that'd be just fine.

Colin had taken his new beach bike to Steve's and he
wandered, taking the long way home, along the Lakeside
Promenade. Gorgeous day, warm not hot, but he knew
that the lake temperature was still in the low sixties. That
lake temperature didn't seem to bother the two young men
swimming, not cavorting, in the water off the end of the
community dock. They had on bathing caps and goggles,
and although Colin couldn't identify them, he knew they
must be his new, seasonal neighbors at Strand's Landing.
He was sure that they weren't Springers. Springers were
often seen wading, fishing, boating, kayaking, but seldom
if ever were they spied swimming. Colin also noticed that
there were two ladies on the community dock. These ladies,
probably part of Eileen's crew, were adjusting the canvas
canopy that covered the platform at the end of the series of
dock pieces that led to that platform. There were pieces of
furniture to be placed just so under that canopy and black
plastic bags surely full of pillows that were there ready to be
strategically placed on said furniture. Other people were
in the area working on their boats. The sooner those boats
were cleaned up, the sooner the captains and crew could
get to the Casino or the Ellicottville Brewing Company in
Bemus Point for lunch served on their waterside decks. Just
as Maple Springs was coming to life, surely Bemus Point,
just down the road or down the lake depending upon your
mode of transportation, was in the throes of a summer

revival.

All the cleaning and revving of boats, etc. did not bother the swimmers who were moving down the lake at a quick pace. For Colin, there seemed to be too much flailing of arms, too much spraying of water surrounding each swimmer. Colin had been a swimmer in high school and although he was devoid of swimming honors, he knew good technique when he saw it and right now he wasn't seeing it. Colin watched for a minute more and then turned and headed down Forest Lawn Avenue thinking that he'd maybe see Ray on his porch. As he neared Ray's and his own home, he could discern music, rhythmic Latin music. It was just past nine o'clock and this loud music was coming from The Landing. The tenants were swimming, why would they head to the lake and leave that loud music playing knowing that it would bother folks? Well, it wasn't as loud as it had been, and Binky wasn't banging on their door to turn it down, so he'd give them a pass. Then he heard loud voices coming from the house. He decided on another pass. It must be visitors because there were just the two renters and those guys knew Binky's music rules. Colin decided that the music, the swimming, the visitors, etc. were all none of his business. He'd keep a furtive watch on the place for his buddy Ben, but these were young adults and he wasn't going to confront them, unless there were valid and compelling reasons to become in loco parentis.

Colin stowed his bike and took his groceries into the

house. He looked out of the kitchen window and saw Ray and his guitar and his earbuds on Brian's back steps. Colin determined that he'd have to go and shake Ray to get his attention. Ray looked like any novice guitar student over there trying to figure out chords on the guitar. There must be an instructional tape involved with those earbuds. It looked like Ray was tapping the guitar to the earbud music. His hands were moving clumsily and Colin had no doubt that Ray was about to make a musical breakthrough, a simple breakthrough but one of enough value to keep Ray moving forward with his musical avocation.

Vonny had left a note saying that she was headed out for paper products and that she'd be home by two o'clock. The note also directed Colin to test the pies and remove them from the oven once they were "ripe", and to be sure to put them on the cooling racks, and turn off the oven and clean up any spots in the oven from over-bubbling pies. When she did arrive home, just after one o'clock, she had two plastic totes filled with big and small plates, bowls and plastic knives, forks and spoons. She had lots of cups too, all sizes. And napkins. Colin kidded Vonny that she had a napkin fetish; napkins of many colors, color combinations and sizes and shapes were displayed on the picnic table under the pavilion. Colin refused to answer when Vonny asked which ones should be used today.

"Come on, honey. You decide," said Vonny. "I selected this huge variety out of cases at the distributer. You narrow it for tonight."

"Against my better judgement, I choose the "Star Wars" model. Both cocktail and dinner size," said Colin.

"We can't use those. I'm saving them for the kids on the 4th of July. Pick again."

"No."

Just then a small Subaru pulled into the driveway and honked its horn. Saved by the honk. Vonny's total attention was shifted to Ronny and Dan as they piled out of their car and gave hugs. Colin took a minute to whisk all the napkins into a plastic bin and put the bin into the shed. He kept out the "Star Wars" napkins, cocktail and dinner size.

The next few hours produced the milieu that Vonny loved to be in. She thrived as mother, homemaker, sage, comforter and all on her own turf, with those that she loved. Ah! No sooner had Vonny gotten the Ronny/Dan laundry started, when into Ray's driveway came a huge silver van. Folks piled out of this vehicle too and with the fence between them, temporarily, there were introductions, expressions of welcome and obvious goodwill and excitement on everyone's part. All nine people, each with guarded expectations, all on their best behavior were ready to mix and mingle. It was a mini-reunion, prelude to that 4th of July extravaganza just a few days away.

Colin usually worried about everybody having a good time, but he soon found that he was not needed in this capacity. At one point in the late evening after a fantastic supper, Colin reviewed in his head the flurry of actions that lead to everyone going to the community dock at sunset and working together to send off "Chinese Sky Candle Lanterns". How could the simple act of sending lit candles inside of a mock paper lantern into the air have such a calming effect on the launchers?

Earlier, as promised, Ray had performed culinary skills at the grill. Later he brought out his guitar and he and Dan, using Vonny's seldom-used eight-string, entertained. Vonny had served as the dinner facilitator, Adam was bartender, Ronny, Tori and Kenzie took charge of the salad, tablecloths and paper products. The young girls were thrilled with the "Star Wars" motif and even had some 'Star Wars' movie music that they played on an iPod just loud enough so that it could drown out any Hispanic music from The Landing if it were to materialize. Colin found a roll of silver crepe paper and some stars leftover from last summer's celebrating and the girls had fun in the decorating mode. Cleanup from dinner was quick; Colin cleaned and retired the grill for the evening and Ronny and Dan cleaned the kitchen. As a group, they decided to wait for a little while before having the Concord grape pie, Vonny's special treat as part of her nurturing role. Only Colin, Vonny and Ronny had ever experienced that variety of pie before and everyone else, except maybe the teenagers, were anxious for the experience. Then everyone "went to their corner" and stowed their gear, some changed, checked their phones and for a bit settled comfortably within the four families that represented the group of nine.

Colin, usually one to foster "a place for everything and everything in its place", knew that it would be a weekend of "stuff everywhere". He'd have to deal with that. He was experiencing a forced sit and trying to relax for a moment when he heard Adam unloading things from the silver van. He hurried next door to help. Those things were actually pieces of exercise equipment to be left at Ray's for his weeks long visit to Maple Springs; mats, hand weights, a press bench, a stationary bike and, best of all, a tandem bicycle were all taken from the van and then moved to Ray's enclosed back porch. Adam and Colin couldn't resist the tandem and took it for a spin around The Springs. Colin had never been on a tandem before and Adam had him experience both the front and back seat.

"Ray has ridden this thing a few times," said Adam once they had returned home. "But I am not sure how comfortable he is on it. He'll probably be more comfortable here because there is so little traffic. I hope that you can be a partner with him if he wants to go riding during the week. I intend to be here on most weekends, Tori too, but I really want Ray to put some miles on this thing even when I am not here. But, if you ever see him going out on it alone, stop him. I'm afraid that his cane will get stuck in the spokes."

Both men were silent for a moment. Then Colin got it and the two of them had a good laugh.

"Ray is a man of great determination and I don't want to stand in his way in any manner. I remember my rehab and recovery after my injury. I wish that I had had the determination that he has. Deanna is great for him too."

Just then Ronny and Dan joined them and asked to take the tandem for a ride. Adam gave quick instructions, supplied them with helmets and they were off down Whiteside Parkway.

"Sorry I forgot about helmets for us Colin. I should keep them in a bag on the handlebars. You and Ray definitely need helmets. He and I used knee and elbow pads for a few turns too. I will leave them for you guys. It looks like Ronny and Dan can handle a bike ride. The roads are in great condition even after your tough winters, and they are flat, my favorite kinds of roads for bike riding. Hills ruin riding for me."

"Hey, you two. I hear you talking about me. Are you plotting," said Ray as he came out of the front door and to the edge of the porch to talk to his Maryland friend and his New York nephew. Colin noticed how the tip of his cane touched the quarter round that was at the edge of the porch and he stopped and talked from there.

"Hey Colin, if you're talking bike business, I was wondering if you have an air pump for tires just in case?" asked Ray.

"Got one and tools to adjust seats, etc. We are set if there are any problems. Adam gave me specifics and warned me about you going off alone. He brought a tire lock to be put on the bike just to keep you in check." They all laughed, then talked specifics concerning safety, a riding schedule, etc.

"Watch out, we're coming in for a landing," shouted Vonny as she and Deanna came flying down the street, thank goodness wearing helmets, and to a perfect stop by the van.

"Ronny and Dan are more interested in skipping stones and so we hijacked the bike. I told them we'd all meet at the community dock just before sunset to let off the lanterns. I think they are just enjoying having nothing to do and being alone. Where are the girls?"

"They walked up to Midway Park. I told them it was closed for the day, but they were going to look around so they know what to expect the next time they come to town," said Ray.

Ray, Adam and Colin organized the back porch for equipment storage and usage and Vonny and Deanna went to make coffee and set up for what Colin called "Pie Time". Deanna sent a text to Kenzie, and Vonny called Ronny reminding them all about "Pie Time". Within minutes, the nine friends and family returned to the pavilion. As expected, the pie with its golden crust and perfectly solidified and yet juicy filling was a hit, even the teenagers thought it terrific. A toast to Vonny was given by Ronny, for Concord grape pie had been her favoritest just as Jack had loved those spinach balls. Then the happy group of nine dispersed to get sweaters and folding chairs and all agreed to meet at the community dock within the half hour for the promised lantern launch.

"Dad, I need to talk to you for a minute," said Ronny. Colin hated nebulous statements like that. During his course as a father he'd been party to a few deep discussions that had started with similar statements.

"Come on, Ron. We'll walk to the creek and you can talk and untangle the knot that you just put in my gut."

"Daddy, what's going on at Kaitlin's house, Strands? When Dan and I were at the beach, these two young men, twenty/twenty-five maybe, were there and in the water and they were on something. Acting all goofy. When they saw us, they toned it down a bit and then left. We started back after them and I saw them go into Strand's. What's happening?"

Colin quickly caught Ronny up with the few details that he knew regarding the wedding, the rental, the tenants, etc.

"I'm on Facebook with Kaitlin, I know about the wedding, but she did not tell me about renting The Landing. She said that she and Gibson would be around at the end of the summer and we hope to get to meet him then, here."

Colin gave Ronny more details regarding the Latino tenants, los muchachos. Colin implored Ronny to keep all this to herself.

"When we passed the Strand's, there was a lot of music

and loud talking to be heard," Ronny continued. "I only saw the two guys at the beach, but there was noise for halfa dozen coming outa that place. Loud music I get. Loud talking and yelling eludes me," said Ronny. "Let's walk by The Landing and see if they are still at it. Let's see if we can get a head count."

No head count was made. The Landing was empty and quiet.

"I bet they are in Bemus. I think there is an Abba tribute band tonight on the floating stage. I will, surreptitiously, check on los muchachos tomorrow. You like that word, surreptitiously? Use it three times and it's yours."

Ronny and her daddy had a good laugh over his efforts to help her increase her vocabulary, a trick he had employed with her ever since she first started talking and boy did she talk early. Ronny and Colin were good friends, shared the love of teaching and had a mutual respect that went beyond father/daughter and teacher/teacher. Colin was so glad to know that she and Dan would be, almost, in residence for the summer.

Colin and Vonny sat on folding sand chairs to enjoy the lantern launch. The "kids" performed the launch with flair and expertise and the Maple Springs Nine, as they had started calling themselves, had a graceful end to the start of a great weekend, summer, lifetime of support and friendship.

CHAPTER 15

Although everyone agreed to "do their own thing" for the rest of the weekend, that proved to be not tenable. Colin used tenable when talking to Ronny and gave her marching orders to make it her own.

Colin awoke to Ray, Kenzie and Tori sitting on a bench in his neighbor's yard close to the Maple Springs Creek that meandered there on its way to the lake. They sat quietly and Kenzie had a huge book across her knees. Ray was talking softly to the girls. They all tilted their heads and soon there was head nodding and big smiles. Colin determined that they were listening for bird songs. The birds nested and multiplied and ate and frolicked along the creek in abundance. Ray, the man with the great bird call clock for instruction, was being the practiced teacher sharing his expertise with his students. Kenzie quickly found the bird they had just identified by song in her picture book and put a sticky note on the page. Colin surmised that they, just Kenzie and Tori for this phase of the lesson, would then try to spot those same birds by plumage, size, color, flutter.

A note on the kitchen counter told Colin that Vonny and Ronny were touring Maple Springs on the tandem and would probably be stopping at Binky's for tea. Dan and Adam had taken the kayaks across the lake for a bagel at Hogan's Hut. Deanna chose to sleep in, but promised fresh baked chocolate chip cookies sometime during the day. Sally Mitchell was expected as was Vicki from *Elegant Edibles* and Eileen was showing up to "answer questions and make everyone happy with the surroundings and the mechanics of Ray's summer abode".

Colin made some quick oatmeal and sat on the front porch in his favorite chair. He bought this oak rocker at the indoor flea market in Hartfield. It was about ten o'clock when he finished reading the Saturday, advertisement-filled *Jamestown Post-Journal*. About that same time the MS9 returned to Ray's and then Sally, Vicki and Eileen all appeared within minutes.

"Daddy, I need to talk to you," said Ronny as she stood by his chair. "Let's walk down Forest Lawn for a minute."

The other seven of the MS9 met up with the three new arrivees and they all went into Ray's house. Lots of business and fun going to happen in there thought Colin, but he was happy to take a walk with Ronny. He just hoped that he didn't miss the freshly baked, or currently baking, chocolate chip cookies.

"Two guys, same two I guess, from Strands, were swimming in the lake this morning. We could see them from Binky's porch." said Ronny. "I may be sounding catty, but it was amateur swimming, lots of arms, lots of foam, no speed, no grace or technique. If these guys are expert swimmers from wherever, they better get a coach, watch some videos on YouTube or something and they better learn el rapido or else there isn't a medal or even a team berth in their future. Are you sure that Mr. Strand knows enough about these guys?"

By this time, Ronny and Colin were in front of The Landing and Ronny said, "Listen to that Dad. They're fighting or something weirder. Let's see if we can figure out how many are in there. There's one car with Florida plates, but look at all the towels on the clothesline. Listen to the Spanglish, if you can sort it out over the music. It's only ten o'clock. Let's hurry on to the lake to see if the two renters are still there."

Colin knelt down and pretended to tie a shoe lace while he gave a quick listen to the noise coming from The Landing. Then Colin and Ronny walked quickly toward the lake. The two young men were still lakeside, but were starting to walk up Forest Lawn back to The Landing. Surely it was the tenants. They had on flip flops and towels over their shoulders. Colin noticed too that they had on board shorts, shorts that went to their knees. Why weren't these swimmers wearing Speedos? Didn't the bulky board shorts impede their speed? Were there Speedos under their board shorts?

"Buenos dias, Senores," said Colin as he and Ronny passed the two young men.

"Allo," the two said in unison and they increased their walking pace as the two groups of two passed each other half way between the lake and The Landing.

As soon as they passed, Colin quickly turned and watched the two walkers from the rear. He couldn't tell if they were wearing two layers of bathing suits.

"Ronny, do you think they have Speedos on under their board shorts?"

"Doubt it, but I bet they have lily white buns under there. Look where the shorts sag, you can see a white line of skin. I'm glad they aren't plumbers," said Ronny.

"Never mind checking buns young lady. You're a married woman."

"What I mean dad is that if they are supposed to be 'men of color' why do they have those sun-deprived tushies?"

"Oh Ronny, I am so glad that you have retained and exercised the humor gene that I so graciously passed on to you."

It was a great father/daughter moment, one of many that the two had shared over the years.

Colin and Ronny arrived back at Ray's just as the other seven and the three newcomers were settling on the porch for fun and cookies.

"I heard the loud music, we all did, and I was wondering if you and los muchachos were 'making nice' like Bernardo warns the Sharks about meeting with the Jets," said Ray.

"Just reconnoitering. We will talk later. We can't make a move without Sergeant Binky. But keep in mind that I always 'make nice,'" rejoined Colin.

The MS9 gang plus three carried on both seriously and silly. Ray had named the group MS9 after a gang of the same name that he had infiltrated and helped to break-up while he was on loan to a swat-team type organization in a large, unnamed city, not Baltimore. Vonny, in mother mode, worried that people might be hungry. In that same role and as a result of preplanning, just after noon, the pizza delivery guy from Coppola's Pizzeria arrived with Calzones and wings. A good time was had by all.

CHAPTER 16

"The weekend really flew by," said Vonny. "It was so good to have the kids, two anyway, home for the weekend. We won't see them again until the 4th when the other four are to be here too. Did Ronny tell you that they wouldn't be here the weekend after the 4th? Someone's getting married in Cleveland.

"I'm so glad that the Baltimore gang was so easy to be with. I learned a lot about Ray from Deanna. She really loves that guy. She and Kenzie have been through a lot too," said Vonny as she sat in the pavilion after having waved to Ronny and Dan until they were out of sight.

"I can't believe that they all want to come back here for the 4th," said Colin. "They left early this morning. It's the last week of school for the girls and they have lots to do. The finals are over, but there is moving-up day and all the other end-of-the-year stuff to be part of. I heard the van leave about six o'clock. Ronny and Dan would have left earlier too, but they still had laundry to fold and the car to pack.

"Adam too was easy to be with. I got lots of tips from him about eating and exercising, and although he didn't ask, I volunteered to be an exercise buddy with Ray. I gotta admit that riding through The Springs on that bicycle-built-for-two is terrific. I got it down and Ray and I have been out twice so I don't think we will have problems," said Colin.

"Ray was a great success at the pool table and with his guitar at Tom's, so I think we know where to find him should we need him in a hurry anytime this summer."

Colin sat with Vonny in the pavilion.

Indeed, it had been a busy weekend and Colin smiled as he thought about the last three days and the fact that no one had gotten on the nerves of anyone else. Lots of together time, alone time and new experiences for most: the tandem, kayaking, Concord grape pie, chicken wings, bird song listening, shopping at Amish craft shops. Colin hated for the weekend to end, but he knew that MS9 would reappear and he was confident that summer would not be boring in Maple Springs. Last summer they had hosted the Ronny/Dan nuptials. This summer Ray would be the focus. Perhaps next year would be typical, whatever typical was.

"Help, I'm being kidnapped by a psycho," it was Ray calling, flying by on the tandem with Sheriff Joe up front.

"Don't try to stop us, or its curtains for all of you," shouted Joe as the bike and riders flew by the O'Briens. The twosome on the tandem got both Colin and Vonny to their feet and to the edge of the road.

"And I thought Ray would be insufferable, would squelch our plans. Don't think me a softie, but with Ray here, I feel like a kid again. I think I missed him. In spite of his 'bottle' and blind problems, he is probably in the best place that he has ever been. I don't mean Maple Springs. I mean the place in his mind; his concept of who he is and how he can function in this world with some grace and purpose. Was that a dorky thing to say?"

Amid a hug, into Colin's ear, Vonny said, "Of course it was dorky. I've come to expect that from you. You're my adorable, dorky lover. Oh, and you have a great sense of humor."

They broke the hug.

"Now," Vonny continued, "get your sneakers on. When those two guys on the bike get back, you're riding me around the 'hood, and I am not peddling at all and I might even take my hands off the handlebars. Hurry up, they can't last long at the speed they were pedaling."

CHAPTER 17

Colin finally got himself settled in an Adirondack chair on the platform at the end of his dock with a small cooler at his feet. He also had a canvas bag filled with four new library books and his safari hat. He loved that hat, bought it in Animal Kingdom at Disneyland. The canvas bag was a necessity. Once he took loose books to the platform and bird poop, wind and his own clumsiness made him have to reimburse the Bemus Point Library for two of the three books he had that day. Earlier he and Vonny had a late breakfast at The Bemus Inn and she went off to work. He went to the library and then returned home. He worked on his "to do list" and now he was on the dock for a mid-afternoon lunch, some good reads and no bogus thoughts to get between him and Sue Grafton. She almost finished the alphabet and I can't even get through "K", thought Colin. Would some stranger please channel Grafton for the "Z" installment?

"Hey mister. They sent me from the library to be sure that you were treating their books in a gentle manner," shouted someone from a small, quiet boat, slowly passing his dock. It was a sheriff's boat and aboard was Sheriff Joe Green and a lady deputy who was at the wheel. Colin was sure that the term "lady deputy" was not at all PC. He'd have to ask Joe for the correct nomenclature for a female who served in the ranks within a sheriff department. He was fairly sure that the word nomenclature would not be part of the job title or job description.

"I'm looking for you," said Joe. "Sit still, I will be right there." Joe, rather Ms. Deputy, pulled up alongside an adjacent dock and Joe jumped onto the dock and came quickly to the second Adirondack chair on Colin's platform. Joe knew from past tries that the water at the end of Colin's dock was not deep enough for tying up a boat.

"Hey Joe. Glad to see ya. Between bikes and boats, you're spending a lot of time in The Springs," said Colin as the two men, friends and onetime co-workers, shook hands.

"I'll talk fast, you know me, because lots of things are happening and I want to be hovering over pieces of this situation as they emerge," Joe began. "So here's the story. I hope you don't know any of this because I have been, legally, keeping details close to the vest. Yesterday when Ray and I gave the tandem over to you and Vonny…God I love that bike…I rushed right off. I knew that you two would take care of Ray and the bike and the helmets. Anyway, I got a call to get to the Marina at Long Point State Park because a body had washed up right in front of the public boat launch site. It was a quiet day at the Marina and so we let people think that we were rescuing a swimmer and not fishing out a cadaver.

"I'm not finished," said Joe purposely raising a hand in the "stop in the name of love" pose a la Miss Diana Ross when he saw Colin's lips start to form a word.

Colin remembered Joe's MO of thinking and talking and segueing, so Colin put on his listening ears as he had been told to do his whole life. During his elementary school years, Colin did more talking than listening and he considered himself the class cut up. He realized as an adult that he was probably ADHD as a kid. That was probably part of the reason for his becoming a special education teacher.

"I'm listening. Honest. Keep going. Don't let the bored look on my face keep you from completing your monologue," said Colin.

As was his habit, Joe continued in an organized, thoughtful manner. "The body hadn't been in the water long, probably three or four days. It rose to the surface as gasses built up. Oops, too much info. Anyway, that body could have gone in the lake almost anywhere, and then depending upon the winds still end up at the Marina. It was a young man. He looked healthy, there were no bumps on his head, no big wounds. The body got thrown around at the shore with waves from passing boats churning the lake, you know. The Coroner, remember Glenn, Glenn Fourtney, he has Juan Doe now. I called him that because he looks Hispanic. Probably shouldn't do that. I mean no disrespect.

"Anyway, when I got home last night after divvying up the duties surrounding the introduction of a dead body into my professional life, I called Ray about future bike rides. I told him I might even bring a kid or two. Ray being in the field, I told him about Juan and he blabbed about the Hispanic muchachos at Strand's. Now, keeping in mind the level of fantastic investigative skills required by my department members, I'd like you to tell me what you know and I will see 1. if Ray was messing with my head, 2. if Ray did not pay attention when you gave him the rundown on why Ben let these guys rent his cottage, or if 3. he erroneously defined himself as a former investigator from Baltimore . Go ahead, it's my turn to listen."

Colin quickly relayed to Joe the specifics concerning the young twosome that was occupying Strand's Landing. Colin repeated the facts just as he remembered them from the conversation that he had had with Ben Strand before los muchachos had arrived. Colin was fairly sure that only he, Vonny, Ray, Ronny-sort-of and now Joe knew these specifics. Colin was fairly sure too that Joe, employing his keeping things close to his vest habit, was mulling and not talking things over with people. The last time Colin and Joe worked together, Joe convened all the people involved with a murder at Maple Springs and the group solved the murder in short order. That culminating meeting gave Colin great respect for Joe and his investigatory and group handling skills.

"Ray had been paying close attention when you relayed Ben Strand's story regarding the summer tenants at The Landing," said Joe. "His recall was good. He also had some insights that he was more than willing to share about the music and the noise, etc."

"So, my friend, you're here soaking up my sun, not drinking my beer 'cuz yur on duty and I dare say that you're finding it difficult to put together a scenario for this crime. Joe, it's early. You haven't even gotten enough vowels or consonants and you're trying to solve the puzzle," said Colin.

"Well, there are no bushes on this dock that's fifty feet out into the lake to beat around, so I will get right to the dilemma. I'm headed to Binghamton, four hours east on 86, for a training on scams and fraud and there are a lot of pieces regarding this cadaver that I need to get organized locally. I got two officers off sick, the 4th comin' up and there will be a whole bunch of high school graduations happening within the next two weeks. Three retirees are coming on board for a few days to get us through this crazy time. Fourtney is really busy, remember there was that apartment house fire up north a couple of days ago, but he's probably going to have results soon that I have to act on," said Joe. He took a pause. "I want to surveil these guys down here, make sure that they don't leave, learn more about them. Any relationship between these boys and the dead man? I'm sure that I can't get a warrant to search The Landing just because the tenants are Hispanic like the cadaver. I'd never even ask Judge Melendez in Dunkirk for that warrant."

"Did you see the cadaver's butt?" blurted Colin.

"What?" asked Joe loudly.

"Butt, ass, hinny, tush, did you see it? Is he a man of color, Juan, or is he tanned, a 'wannabe' Hispanic."

Colin jumped right into telling Joe how he and Ronny had gone looking for the Hispanics in residence and had found lots of towels, board shorts and white butts.

"I'm calling Glenn," said Joe and he stood, dialed his cell phone and talked real fast. "You heard me, I said butt, butt, I said butt. Just look, will ya? Put the phone down and look. I'll hang on."

Colin and Joe waited while the coroner got 'up close and personal' with Juan who turned out to be John.

"My mind is trying to piece this all together," said Joe. "…guys pretending to be Hispanic, tanning sessions, could have died hair. I should have asked Glenn to check on his roots. Is this cadaver one of the twosome at Strand's? No! Last night when I called, Ray told me about the Hispanic guys at Strand's and said they were out walking around. Their voices were moving around, sometimes on their porch, sometimes in the street. Ray was on his porch, it was late. He said he heard two voices, whispering, but arguing. Why argue/whisper outdoors?

"I gotta go Colin. Thanks for your input. I'm meeting Ray at Tom's. He's teaching Eileen to play pool. Can you believe it? Join us. Three o'clock. I leave from there on 86 to Binghamton. Meet us. Gotta go."

Colin sat for a few minutes and watched Joe and the deputy quickly leave the dock and go tearing down the lake toward Long Point State Park where Joe must have left his car. As it turned out, Colin would see a lot of that deputy, Vanessa, over the summer. She had been hired specifically to patrol the lake and to help boaters. She was also supposed to make sure that her presence would be a deterrent for those bad boy boaters that appear regularly.

Colin gathered his belongings and headed home after stowing the Adirondack chairs on the shore back from the water. Joe had surely made him even more curious about the young men at Strands. Did they know the John Doe? Had that dead boy visited in The Springs at some point? The body was found not so far away. Was there a boating accident? No wounds on the victim. Was Colin's role of deputy to reoccur in the very near future?

Joe had just taken Colin into his confidence on the dock. Joe had done that once before when his youngest son, Tone, was born. That time too, Joe was out of his jurisdiction. Colin had, through quirks of proximity, intellect and necessity, proved to be a valuable team player when a murder in Maple Springs needed to be understood and solved. Colin was casually deputized, although he took that title very seriously. Was Joe thinking of having Colin join as part of an investigating team again? Colin quickly decided not to count his unhatched chickens.

When Colin got home, he got out his beach bike and started leisurely riding around the block. He told himself that he was needing some exercise and that he was part of a neighborhood watch team. After all, Ben Strand had also asked him to semi-surveil. Colin knew that he was just being curious, not being nosey. His first turn around the block using four different streets told him that it was a very quiet day in The Springs. He was fairly sure that his recently returned summer resident neighbors were in one of three places: Home Depot, Wegmans Market or in their boats on the lake. Driveways, porches and yards were empty. Some folks might have only been in residence for a day or two and then returned home. They'd be back this coming weekend. This was the common summer homesteading pattern although there were some folks who stayed the entire summer and then there were the yearrounders among which Vonny and he were counted.

There was no one, no music, no loud talking at The Landing. At Ray's, there was no one on the porch. Ray could have been on the stationary bike on the back porch, or just inside somewhere on the computer. He had software that turned the visuals on the screen into audio. Colin wasn't exactly sure how that was at all possible. Ray offered to give him a demonstration and they were going to sing together using some website Ray used to help himself learn lyrics and chords simultaneously. Colin had dared to sing with Ray at Tom's over the weekend and frankly it wasn't awful. Ray offered to work with Colin and the two of them were going to do a medley of patriotic songs at the 4th of July picnic/family reunion extravaganza. Ray was excited for the challenge. Colin not so much.

The third time around the block, when Colin was sure that no one was at home, Colin stopped in front of The Landing's driveway. He pretended to check the chain on his bike. He checked the tires for air loss and he repositioned the seat ever so slightly by hitting it with the palm of his hand.

No one is home for sure thought Colin. The porch is a mess, garbage cans are overflowing, lots of towels on the line. The boys could be swimming or at the laundromat in town. Or they might be sleeping. They had better make sure that their garbage is in the cans with the lid tightly sealed or else the raccoons and other critters will stop to dine and they are not neat eaters. Rodent table manners are terrible. What do you expect from rodents? Oh, and crows are the ultimate sloppy scavenger. Crows also spread non-edible garbage in a wide circle around a garbage can.

When Colin arrived home, he stowed his bike and ate the lunch that he had not even touched when he was on the dock. He then sat at the kitchen table to listen to the eight messages that were on his answering machine. He had only been gone for about one hour and all eight calls must have come in during that time. He carefully made sure to get each caller's name, to jot down their telephone number if they left one and to properly characterize the caller's message. In the past he had been accused of "editorializing" or "trivializing" messages that he interpreted in his own vernacular after switching said messages from the audio on the answering machine to the visual on a note pad. Colin did not agree that he was snide, that was the word that someone had used, but he nonetheless became a better message transcriber. He wrote the list carefully for surely the calls would be of interest to Vonny:

Dianne Warren…I won't be there till after the 4th this year, call me when you get a chance, new knees are great, greet Vonny for me

Strange lady with an incoherent message… "ugh, the state is here, if I'm not home by midnight, send Sheriff Joe to spring me"

Ben Strand…Hope all is calm in The Springs…is The Landing still there?…I will call later, we are off to a cake tasting session…will Kaitlin and Gibson agree on a cake?, they haven't agreed to much else

R & D…thanks mom & dad…weekend was great, love Uncle Ray, the 4th will be a blast, love you, miss you, see you soon

Verizon…have we got a deal for you!

Discover Card…we have lowered our interest rates for veteran customers like you, call the number on the back of your card and ask for Meghan

Vonny, its' Cousin Gordon…calling to RSVP for the 4th, four of us including Leah's new boyfriend… don't ask. BeeBee is making au gratin (or did he say rotten) potatoes. Call if you must.

Yo Mamma... "*I took the liberty of calling folks I
was sure were invited for the 4th and I am organizing
the food (pot luck for me is pot unlucky)...all yesses.
Ray? My stars.*" *(accurate quotes)*

Once he had the calls all carefully noted, Colin erased
the messages and made a return call to only one of the eight
callers.

"Hello this is Veronica O'Brien, Director of Social Work.
How may I help you?"

"Hello this is Colin O'Brien, husband of the director of
social work. You can help me in more ways than you know.
What are you wearing?"

"Good afternoon, sir. I am keeping my business demeanor and I won't be answering rude questions AND I
won't be laughing at your charming sense of humor, as if I
ever did."

"Oh you did, you should, how can you not? Humor is a
wonderful source of relief and decompression. As a social
worker you should know that. How's it going there? Got
your message. Sorry, Joe is headed to Binghamton for a
conference and won't be home till Thursday. If you're not
home by Thursday, I promise to send him to spring you."

Vonny found herself laughing at Colin's charming sense
of humor. How could she not?

Before they hung up amid kissing sounds and the promise of "chilled wine awaiting", Vonny assured Colin that her
office was unscathed in spite of a drubbing by inspectors.

In fact, the whole place was humming along in spite of the inspection team overseeing and shadowing everyone and every procedure in the facility.

"It's a new one day inspection and they said that they would be done soon and we would have an exit meeting before they left. I like this one day bit. We're having dinner with their survey team and our administrative team during which we hear the good and the bad. Talk about an appetite suppressant. Then I will be home. If I don't have deficiencies, I'm taking tomorrow off. Where are we going to celebrate? Where are you taking me to dinner? What are you buying me at Skillman's?"

Colin did not answer the three final questions. Instead, he wished her good luck, told her not to worry about his dinner and he reminded her that he loved her and that she was the best social worker that he had ever bedded.

Vonny found herself laughing at Colin's charming sense of humor, again. How could she not?

CHAPTER 18

"Hey there Mr. O'Brien. Good day ta ya. What'll it be?" It was Eileen Miller, property manager extraordinaire, bartending at Tom's. "Surprised? Don't worry, I got barkeep skills, but don't much use them for drawing beer and popping cheesy popcorn. I can make you a pink squirrel if you'd like. Bet one of them has never been made in this place. How 'bout a fuzzy navel, or an apricot sour? Wait, Tom probably don't have the ingredients. On tap we have, Yangalang, Budlight, Labatts and a couple fancy beers from Southern Tier Brewery. What's your poison?"

Before Colin named his poison, his mind was racing to figure out why Eileen was tending bar, but then he named his poison and quizzed Eileen about her what-looked-like-it-might-be-a-part-time job.

"I'm taking Whitey's place and he is out on his huge, new, riding lawnmower at the houses that I landscape for. He can finish in half the time that it would take me. He'd rather be outdoors and I love hanging around here. And I get all the cheesy popcorn I want."

Eileen was a character. She had a sketchy past, but had been embraced by the whole of Maple Springs as she got her life together and made a place for herself in this world. Currently she was indispensable to many families and she earned their respect with her solid work ethic, her honesty and the fact that she "had skills". Everyone loved Eileen.

Eileen served Colin's poison and, probably because he was the only customer in the place, they had a calm and personal conversation: Ray's settling in, the upcoming 4th, shades of mulch, who provides the best tree service in the area.

"Hey, I just thought! How's Ray getting here? I walked, but I could have driven him," said Colin.

"He'll be along. He's gotten hisself here before. He has a talking watch, a cane and two good feet. I can't be worrying 'bout him," replied Eileen.

Just then the bell that, sometimes, rings when a patron enters, rang and in lurched Raymond McGill. "Top o' the marnin' to ya Miss Eye-leen. It be Raymond McGill come for to be givin' you lessons on the emerald green table that elevates the cunning of the common man and makes fools of the gentry. Are ya ready sweet Eye-leen?"

"He's your kin Colin, why didn't you never develop to be the charming man that he is?" asked Eileen.

"Colin, I didn't know you were here. Come on now Eileen, don't take us down that nature/nurture path. If we're here for pool, then pool it be."

Eileen deserted the bar, found a cue she favored and the lessons were in gear. Ray sat in close at the table's end where the rack of 15 balls had been placed. Colin and his Labatt were the only audience and both Colin and Eileen learned a lot about style, stance, the rhythm of the game and the intense need for the table to be placed just so; the table should be perfectly level and the felt and the balls need be perfectly clean.

With the first break of those errant orbs, Ray was "into it". He tuned into what was rolling around the table and he knew when a ball was sunk. He asked Eileen what she was contemplating and if he thought she was rushing it, he'd say things like, "keep standing and thinking, you're not ready to shoot". But his past life skills and his love of the game only took him so far.

"Ray, I'm in jail, now what?" said Eileen at one point.

"Where's your bank? Where's your next best shot? Think. Talk to whitey. Pool's a thinking man's game," Ray replied.

The lesson moved quickly, there was lots of talk, there was laughter and sage advice; "quit talkin' and start chalkin", "follow through, it's like pitching".

Just as the pool lesson was winding down, Whitey returned and assumed his position behind the bar.

"They are almost finished," Colin said. "Eileen was keeping us unruly folk under control. Hey, I was wondering if you mow at Strand's Landing? I know the Strands aren't going to be around till late in the season. Brian too and I just got a message from Dianne Warren and she will be up to the lake late. You mow for her?" Colin asked Whitey.

"I mow for lots of locals. Eileen does too. We often share the work so that we don't get behint. Some folks

NEED that lawn mown each week, or else, and others just wanna to be able to wade through and not bump into an old bike that fell over. So it's yes to Strand and Warren and this year we have Brian 'cause he's got a tenant," said Whitey.

"There's that tenant over there with Eileen, but then, you probably already knew that. He's my uncle, betcha didn't know that. If you get behind, I can do Brian's lawn when I do mine. Back to Strand's for a second. You met his tenants? We hear them a lot, loud music, but don't see them much. You? Sometimes they're swimming in the lake. Must still be pretty cold."

"Messy lot they are. I had to pick up all kinds of stuff, mostly paper and cans an' junk, before I could mow. Don't like to mow something into a thousand pieces. Didn't talk to them, but they were on the porch roof layin' in the sun the whole time I was there. Young. Dark, not black, but dark, probably Hispanic. They all had headphones on, listening to music I guess. I just mow, don't get nosey. Ben Strand pays for mowin' not inspectin' or baby sittin'. Eileen says she is to be repairin' if there's a need for that sorta thing. You getting friendly with them? They're gonna be here for a few more weeks, till the end of July I think," said Whitey as he tied a not-too-white apron around his ample girth and began to wipe the bar insuring that he met the cleanliness standards that Tom's was noted for.

"I've seen the boys. Ray and I call the los muchachos," said Colin. "We hear them and their music sometimes, but pretty much they keep to themselves, or they're in town or swimming. They're athletes. They're supposed to be getting ready for meets or even the Olympics at home, wherever. They make a lot of noise for two people."

"Two? You gotta be kiddin," said Whitey. "Two?"

"You think there's more? Ben Strand said there would be two, two swimmers, but if you think there are more, I can see it. There is a lot of noise for two, lots of garbage and towels too, but I have never seen more than two of them at a time," said Colin.

Both men were quiet for a bit. Whitey went to the popcorn machine for a basket of the house special, cheesy popcorn, and set another Labatt in front of Colin.

"This beer is on the house. Actually I'll set up the whole place. Ray doesn't drink, right? Neither does Eileen. My offer stands," Whitey said and then in a loud voice he announced, "Drinks are on the house!"

"Back to The Landing for a minute," said Colin as he tried to steer Whitey back to the topic that he was most interested in. "Did you hear the Landing tenants talking? Was it Spanish or what? I'm not being nosey. Ben did call and asked me to keep my distance, but to nonetheless keep an eye on the place."

Colin was carefully feeling his way through this conversation with Whitey. Colin didn't want to mention that los muchachos were the children of South American leaders or opposition leaders or drug dealers or whatever. Colin was also careful not to mention that a body, a maybe Hispanic body, had washed up at Long Point.

"You've heard my lawnmower. I hear no one, nothing. I had on earphones just like the sun bunnies on the porch roof. I know nothing and I want to keep it that away."

Almost simultaneously the pool lessons ended, Sheriff Joe Green entered and Eileen exited Tom's headed to the Maple Springs Inn to put in place newly arrived striped awnings that would surely bring a bit of pizzazz to the curbside appeal of the Inn.

Colin, Ray and Joe and a pitcher of Sprite, and cheesy popcorn, and Colin's third Labatt, convened at the table in the corner farthest from the bar. Whitey busied himself in the kitchen and after perfunctory greetings, Joe got down to business.

"Not much new from the coroner. You were right about John Doe being friends with Miss Clairol. That dye job and the white butt lead me to believe that Juan is John, but also a Juan wannabe. Toxicology reports indicate…I like saying that…toxicology reports indicate that the body was three to four days old when we found it at Long Point. He died with lungs full of Lake Chautauqua swill, but bruises on the upper torso indicate that he might have been held under water. There was probably a struggle of some intensity according to Glenn," said Joe.

The three experienced investigators sat for a quiet minute contemplating the venom and strength involved with a forced drowning.

"Hey Mr. O.," it was Whitey beside their table breaking the silence. "I shoulda told ya about the ruckus with some Hispanic guys here a few days ago. They was out back throwin' shoes and it got loud and rough. Tom sent them away after confiscating the shoes and told them to come back when they could be civil. Above all else, this joint is a civil establishment, ya know. They weren't inside long so I didn't hear talkin', but they ordered cervases and all had New York State drivers licenses. No, before you ask, I do not remember names or cities. Out back they was quiet at first and then there was cursin', loud cursin'. They were just yellin', not words, and then, because of Tom, they were gone. I figure with that cursin' that those were the first English words those boys learned. I also figured that they was passin' through, but then they went down Summit into The Springs. Could be the boys at the Landing. Don't know, ya know. That's all I know. Bye. Another round, Mr. O.? Pitcher, Sheriff?"

"Have another beer, Colin. I'll be the designated driver," said Ray.

"We are all set," said Joe. Whitey returned to the bar. "Okay fellas, I have to get on the road and make it to Binghamton for an eight o'clock address by some big lawyer from Albany. He's talking about scams. There's a ton of them especially perpetrated on senior citizens like you two. Before I go, I want to leave you two with marching orders, but only if you're game. What do you say?"

Ray and Colin, without hesitation, agreed to at least listen and then they'd decide upon their gameness.

"Here's all I ask," started Joe. "Just semi-monitor the comings and goings of the guys in The Landing. License numbers of cars bringing guests would be good, or their license number if they have a car. Bike rental info too."

"They have had a car there. It had a Florida plate," said Colin. "Remember, the guy that vouched for them to rent from Ben was a lawyer in Florida. If need be, we can get info from Ben in Florida, but then there might be lawyer/client confidentiality business to deal with. Haven't seen a car the past few days. They had bikes from the bike rental in Bemus I'd guess and once or twice there was a taxi over there. I thought they had the cab because no one was in condition to drive and they came home from the Casino or from somewhere in Mayville. I really wasn't paying much attention, but I will be en garde, my capitaine…that wasn't Spanish, was it? Sorry."

"Joe, we have no status to be your eyes and ears in The Springs," said Ray. "I know all the details for citizen's arrests. I can even read Miranda rights. I know that eye witnesses are welcomed, even a narc embraced, but to have vulnerable citizenry thrown into the investigatory machinations of a highly trained policing unit can be risky. How can we possibly be emboldened and efficient without the comfort and status of being a deputy. Oh, grant us that status, give us the authority to act in your stead. Then and only then may we flourish."

Joe, obviously in on the joke, couldn't keep up his part of the scenario and he began laughing. Ray joined him in laughter. And soon Colin, remember he just had three beer, laughed loudest of all.

CHAPTER 19

When Colin returned home, he opted for a brief nap and Ray sat on his own porch, as he said, "to read the paper". Ray had been keeping a busy schedule with visitors and working with Sally Mitchell and getting the lay of the land and he was feeling that he had lost track of what was, as he said, "transpiring on the planet". Ray thought it a necessity to "catch up". Colin, remember he just had three beers, saw the nap as a necessity.

When Colin awoke, it was six o'clock, but he quickly remembered that Vonny had a date with the state so there was no push for dinner plans. Did cheesy popcorn count as a healthy, low carb lunch?

"Colin! Colin! Duty calls," said Ray through the kitchen screen door. "The alleged perps are on the move. Come, gimme your arm. We're going for a walk."

Colin followed directions and within seconds he and Ray, wearing sunglasses and holding his cane in the fold position, were slowly walking by Strand's.

"What do ya think of my disguise, Colin?" said Ray. "I'm hoping to throw off the boys and get them to thinking that I'm a poor, old blind man to be pitied."

"You hit all those points, Ray," said Colin. "Now what's got you motivated here?"

"I was reading the paper, you know, but was really listening. Now I know how a Peeping Tom operates, but I'm an Eaves Dropping Ernie. They were arguing about time in the water, I think. At first they were inside and I could get a lot of words in English... 'practice', 'duty', 'promise'...then when they came out onto the porch, it got all Spanglish and fast so I missed most of what they said. But for sure, it was an argument; the lazy versus the inspired. Then the voices faded and I think that they were headed to the lake. So let's go find them, maybe meet with them and remember what Grandma Kitty taught us... "Make new friends, but keep the old..."

"One is silver and the other gold," ended the song in a lovely, harmonic duet.

As Ray and Colin arrived at the green space on the lakefront, an area for homeowners to share and respect, the two young men were slipping into the water at the end of Strand's dock. They quickly began swimming, actually demonstrating valid swim strokes that were allowing them to cover considerable distance.

Colin gave Ray a verbal picture of the area and the activity of the boys.

"What'd they leave on the dock?" asked Ray. "Any pockets to rifle or phones to borrow?"

"No," answered Colin. "It looks like t-shirts, towels and hats and flip flops."

"What are you two fine gentlemen doing on such a lovely evening here in 'the beauty spot on Lake Chautauqua'?"

said Binky King as she, and Elgin, walked up behind the two newly created Chautauqua County Deputy Sheriffs.

"Gees, Binky. Don't sneak up on a fella like that," said Colin almost aflutter.

"I heard her coming Colin," said Ray. "If she had not spoken, her signature perfume would have given her away. Mornin' Miss Claudia. Lovely to be in your company."

"Love this man. Elgin, it's Uncle Ray. Come say hello," said Binky aka Claudia.

As though it were a staged maneuver, Elgin's tiny, adorable head squeezed its way from between the shoulder straps of his secure abode.

"He's so happy to see you Raymondo. Your little friend Fluffy misses you. Come sit on the porch, it's too late for tea, as is our usual, but we have a fancy schmancy coffee machine that Bernie loves to play with and we can have a dark roast, chocolate infused, machio, thingio that only Bernie can negotiate. No saying no. Give me two minutes to slice the banana/peanut butter bread, your favorite Raymond, and we'll 'jaw' as you so elegantly put it." And she was off to slice, prod Bernie, fluff pillows and secure Elgin into what was probably his own private, highly decorated summer cottage room.

"Looks like you two are simpatico here," said Colin.

"Right you are. She is a dear. Best part is, she has a designer friend in Baltimore that she is going to hook me up with and we, Deanna and I, can buy new stuff, showroom stuff for peanuts for our new house. Deanna has to pick it out. All I get is the butt test and the sniff test. Enough! We are on duty. Let's go to Claudia's and we can quiz her about the boys. She sees them in the lake all the time. The lady is savvy.

"What's going on now? Are they swimming or goofing around? Are they wearing goggles or swim caps? Board shorts or speedos? Are they going far in one direction or are they going back and forth? Come on Annie, I need your help."

"Annie, Claudia, Fluffy," said Colin incredulously. "I get Fluffy and assume that Claudia is Binky's real name, but Annie?"

"Let that be a challenge to you," said Ray as he turned right on Lakeside Promenade and headed to Binky's, a place he certainly had a familiarity with. Colin, on the other hand, although he had been in The Springs for five years, had never had the pleasure of setting foot into what he was sure would be an over-the- top, highly decorated, electronically infused, right-out-of-*Architectural-Digest* lake home.

"I must commend those young men. They have been in the lake, I hardly put my toe in there, just about every day," started Binky.

Ray got himself comfortable in a cushy outdoor, rain-resistant chair. He then encouraged more conversation regarding the comings and goings of los muchachos from Strand's Landing.

"Don't think me weird," continued Binky, "but I have named those young men Carlos and Miguel and as I said they come every day. Some days I am not sure if it is them, but I am not close enough to tell. One day Bernie…hey Bernard where are our Machiolottios?...he said he bet their names were Amid or Amir, but no, I heard them at The Landing. They are Hispanic. Anyway, every day, not at a regular hour, they appear and swim or tan. I don't get the tanning. That isn't going to increase speed. What I think they really need is a coach, someone on the pier correcting strokes, or counting for breathing, you know, coaching. Bernie says I should butt out…BERNIE!"

Bernie appeared and served syrup-like expresso coffee in small cups decorated with exotic birds. So much for the highly touted macchio whateverio. Bernie left the coffee press that he had used to make the expresso and a basket of neatly cut slices of banana/peanut butter bread. He explained that he was not being rude, but that he had to go inside because he was participating in virtual home tours in California and he needed to be diligent. There were several new developments of high-end houses that he and Binky were hoping to be awarded the contract to decorate. "I must remain vigilant," he said with a flourish as he left the porch.

"He's such a poop," said Binky. "Now, what else do you

need to know and why are you two being such nosy Rosies?"

Colin jumped right in to provide a nebulous answer to keep Binky out of the fray.

"Ben Strand called and asked me to keep a furtive eye on the place. He's protecting his investment in the cottage. He does not know, has never met, these renters. I'm just being neighborly."

Ray concurred with Colin and then steered his friend Claudia back to talking about the swim practices that she observed almost daily.

"Yes, they do swim far AND they go across the lake, east to west and back, instead of going north to south. I worry about boaters or tubers or skiers not seeing them, but so far so good. When I said that I wasn't sure that it was always them, I guess that I was thinking that sometimes one is tall and the other short and then the next day they are both tall or both short. Some days they are in the sun or the sun's in my eyes, other times it's later in the day or it's not so bright, so ignore me. It's two young Hispanic swimmers getting on with their program.

"One day," Binky went on, "I took them some fried cakes that I made from a recipe I found on line at a Spanish recipe site. They are called churros and are like fritters, sort of. Easy to make, a Hispanic favorite and I thought the boys might be homesick for a typical dessert and so I made and took. One of them, my Miguel I think, came to the door and I presented the churros and he said 'gracias senorita'. I took that as a compliment. I said that I hoped that he would enjoy them and share them with his friend, his amigo. He went back in and that was that. I stood on the porch for a minute adjusting my Elgin and I could hear talk inside, sounded like more than two voices. Then I thought it was them watching the Spanish channel, channel ocho, and enjoying one of those novella patellas on TV, or whatever, that are so popular. That was my last outreach to the Hispanic community. Here that is. At home we have lots of friends, workers and neighbors of the Hispanic persuasion. They are folks who are ethnically focused."

Colin and Ray took in all of Binky's perceptions. "Binky, you have a great eye and a kind heart. I think that you are the only one who has driven up to The Landing in a welcome wagon. We'll have to try that, don't you think, Ray?" said Colin.

CHAPTER 20

Ray and Colin dined on a frozen Paul Newman pizza as an appetizer and had Ben & Jerry's Chunky Monkey as their main course. They were having coffee, plotting and planning and were just about ready to go inside to Ray's computer. They were going to set a repertoire of songs to practice for the July 4th family reunion/picnic when Vonny drove into Ray's driveway.

"Wine, I remembered the wine," yelled Colin, up and moving. "Ray entertain the Mrs. while I get her vino. She's had a busy day. Don't expect civility."

"Colin you sweetheart," started Vonny. "I had a great day, no deficiencies, got tomorrow and Wednesday, maybe Thursday, off and Amy at work invited me to go stay with her in a condo at Chautauqua. The OT/PT department had no deficiencies too, so she's off. It's a freebee because she has an aunt that owns the condo, but won't be there for a week or more. The condo has a pool, a health spa and we can see the performers on the stage at the Amphitheater from her balcony. Can I go? Please! Please!" said Vonny, as though she had to ask.

Colin indeed did get Vonny the wine. Ray and Colin stuck with the coffee. Vonny talked and talked and laughed and bragged and talked and talked. She also helped with the selection of reunion songs, but before Colin and Ray started to sing, for she knew what to expect, she trudged home.

Colin took it seriously when Ray had offered singing help, but Colin did not want to use the term "singing lessons" for some reason. Before the actual instructions began, they finalized a reunion play list which consisted pretty much of songs that were familiar to both musicians.

"You just can't mess up a song like *This Land is Your Land*," said Ray. "We got this gig in the bag."

Colin wasn't so sure.

Shortly after the rehearsal got underway, with little vocalization actually having taken place, there was the sound of a loud car muffler and then loud talking from the passengers in the delinquent vehicle. The singing help ceased. Ray's living room light was extinguished and the deputies slipped out onto the porch to sit in silence and darkness.

"Yikes," whispered Colin. "It's really dark out here."

"Always is," was Ray's obvious reply.

On Ray's porch there was no more talking, whispering or singing until after the offensive vehicle left the street and the offending voices were stilled within The Landing.

"I'm glad that that mini-noise-fest is over," said Ray. "And I'm glad that I wasn't depending upon that scene to give me any insight into what's really happening at The Landing. What'd you absorb?"

"We'll, here's a play-by-play from my viewing of the scene," said Colin.

"Rub it in, you creep," was Ray's obvious reply.

Not losing a beat, Colin went on, "When the car stopped, I couldn't understand any actual words, that damn muffler, but the car's interior light told me that a girl was driving. I mean a female. A senorita if I'm not mistaken. Three, you heard me, three guys ungracefully exited the car and were up the steps and into the house. The motion detector light by the front door went on and I could tell it was the regulars over there. I'm pretty sure about that. All were about the same height and build. The car was just about out of sight when the boys were fully inside. Got nothing else."

"Three you say," said Ray. "Three. Does that mean that there has always been three there, but they never let us see more than two at a time. That would compute with Binky's viewing of them as swimmers...tall one day, short the next. What were they wearing? Did they have on hats? Were they drunk? It's early, they must have started drinking at happy hour. Home early because they are in training I bet."

"You did it again, all those questions. Shorts and t-shirts, no hats. I bet they were in Bemus either on the Lenhart porch, the dock at The Fish or the porch at the See-Zurh House. It's easy to start early on a summer day in Bemus," answered Colin.

The Maple Springs contingent of the Chautauqua County Sheriff's Department sat silently for a while.

"I better go home," said Colin. "You need help cleaning up? What have you got planned for tomorrow? When we gonna start singing out loud? How do you like all these questions?"

"I love them. They make me feel needed. They make me feel that I have contributions to make to the world and in this case the wonderful world of criminal investigation. As Sally Field puts it, 'you like me, I can tell you really like me.'"

"I'm outta here," said Colin, and indeed he was.

CHAPTER 21

The flurry of activities at the O'Brien's house began early on Tuesday morning. It was too early for Colin. By 7:30, Vonny was on the road to pick up her friend Amy with the goal of being in the pool at the Chautauqua Sunrise Condominiums on the grounds of the Chautauqua Institution by ten o'clock. The Institution, just across the lake from Maple Springs, was world famous for its unique mix of performing and visual arts, lectures, concerts, interfaith worship and programs and recreational activities. Its jammed-packed, nine week, summer schedule of the arts and current world affairs lecturers, brought guests (the Institution did not use the term tourist) from all over the world. It also brought speakers, entertainers, leaders and various luminaries from all over that same world. Colin summarized the Institution with his oft used phrase... "so much to do, so little time, so little money". Chautauqua guests were easily and genuinely engrossed with the "Chautauqua experience" and in the form of jobs, visitor dollars brought into the community and the guarantee of finding a place on the map for Chautauqua County, the Institution always proved to be an instigator. Most evenings when traffic on the lake was slow, or at least quiet, the chiming from the Miller Bell Tower at the waterfront on the Institution grounds could easily be heard at The Springs. On most days the Tower itself could be seen from the O'Brien's porch. Colin and Vonny were not regular Chautauqua visitors, but when they did attend a play, concert or lecture, they were sure to enjoy their visit. Just 2.2 miles from home, across Lake Chautauqua, was the site where the world of culture came to spend nine weeks each summer.

Just as Vonny's car was out of sight, the telephone rang.

"Hi Colin, it's Amy from work, I hope Vonny hasn't left yet."

"Just hit the road. Is there a problem?" asked Colin.

"I think there is a problem. I haven't got a key for the condo. Aunt Jessie forgot to send it along. I don't know where to park. Can I even drive on the grounds? What if the utilities aren't hooked up? Do I, we, have to pay a gate fee? I'm a mess," admitted Amy.

"You sound like my uncle with all those questions. I got your drift. Vonny will be at your house soon. Put your stuff in her car and get to the main gate at the Institution. The guy who runs the whole place, I call him the Mussolini of Chautauqua Institution, because he keeps everything running on time, he lives here at The Springs. He's the operations manager and he has a wad of keys on his belt that must weigh 20 pounds. I bet one of those keys will get you into your Aunt's condo. He can help with all your other concerns too. But I need to call him before he heads to work. Vonny knows him and his wife well. His name is Doug. Tell her to look for him at the gate. Hang up, stop worrying, have fun."

After getting Amy's cell phone number, Colin quickly hung up the phone and then called Mussolini and luckily he hadn't left for work. All of Amy's concerns were not to be of concern. Doug would be to on the job before the ladies arrived and he'd meet them at the gate. He also offered to provide a welcoming fruit basket and he had a book of coupons that offered free ice cream cones, buy-one-get-one-free meals and even discounts in gift shops.

"You're a pal, Doug. Let's hope we can help you guys out some time," said Colin and he and Doug quickly hung up so that Doug could get to work on time.

With Amy and Vonny assured of the getaway that they were hoping for, Colin made a bowl of oatmeal and went out to eat on the porch and to read the day's attempt at "Covering The Way You Live" on the part of the *Jamestown Post-Journal.* Colin looked first over at Ray's to see if there was any life in the cottage. Ray was sitting on the porch in the same chair that he had been in when Colin had left him last evening.

"Ray, Ray, what's happening? You in there? You awake?" blurted out Colin as he, oatmeal in hand, hurried to Ray's porch and up the steps.

Ray startled. That was the first time Colin had seen that reaction. Ray had obviously been asleep and Colin broke that hold on him and Ray jumped, grabbed the arms on his chair and actually let out a squeal of a sort. "I'm good! I'm good! Dozed for a second there, but I'm good. Sorry if I scared you," said Ray.

"Sorry too if I scared you. You weren't there all night, were you? Weren't out here in the dark all night," said Colin. "Don't answer that, I'm having a déjà vu. You need anything?"

"Thanks, Colin. I am fine. I'm having a déjà vu too. Remember when we were kids and sleeping out in the screen porch at Grandma Kitty's and that family of raccoons joined the sleep out. I was under the covers with a flashlight and a comic book and mama raccoon and three babies came under for story hour. I screamed, like a girl as I remember, and you were right there and scooped all four of them critters up in my blanket and dumped them out over the back fence. Then to just be mean, or so I thought at the time, you made me stay out and sleep on the porch, after you barricaded the screen door. It's like getting back on that horse that throws you. I remember that like it was yesterday. I don't think I ever thanked you for that valuable life lesson. Belated thanks."

Colin began quickly eating his oatmeal. "Don't want this 'hot bowl of delicious old fashioned goodness' to get cold," said Colin.

"I was out here for the better part of the night," said Ray after a few moments of respectful silence. "Sometimes I just don't sleep. Deanna says my circadian rhythms are off. During that sleeplessness last night, I listened for action at

The Landing. Not much. Someone brought out garbage. Midnight or so. Same person fell back up the steps and another someone came out to help him. Lots of whispering. They were on the front porch and I assumed that the motion sensor had turned on the light, so I boldly got up and Buddy, that's what I call my cane in private, and I took a walk down Forest Lawn. I was sure that they'd see me and say holla or something. When they didn't, I stopped in front of the Landing, it's just 27 paces from my bottom step, and I said, 'Is someone there? I hear someone. Can someone give me direction please? I live at 4790 on Whiteside Parkway. I got disoriented. Is someone there?' My poor-old-blind-man-to-be-pitied disguise worked and one of the tenants came to me and gave me his arm and kept saying "aqui,aqui" as he pretty much dragged me to the railing on the steps here and he said "buenas noches, Senor" and he made a quick retreat. So Colin, one deputy to another, what do you think I learn from that exchange, that interaction?"

"I am stunned that you so surreptitiously put yourself out there like that," said Colin accusingly. "And as for what do I think you learned, I've haven't the foggiest. Did you learn anything?"

"I learned that the boys are about five foot seven or eight and that they are young, strong and that they were exhibiting drunken behavior last night. When I took the guy's arm, I pulled him in close and his arm was strong, skin tight and smooth. We were shoulder to shoulder so he is my height. You said that the guys that came home were all about the same size. That got me thinking about Binky's thinking that the guys were of varying heights on varying days, so I called Joe, he put his number in my phone, and he called Glenn and had him call me. I was thinking that if the cadaver was a Landing tenant, that he would have been the tall one. Guess what! Here's something else I learned... don't throw yourself into a Sheriff Joe investigation without his permission or direction, or if you do, don't tell him about it. Anyway, Glenn did check on the cadaver's height and he called me. Six foot one. He was the tall one, and I think that might help to prove Binky right about size variations."

"They are probably trying to make us think that there are just two guys living there. Maybe Ben rents by the person," said Colin. "Ben said that two were coming to rent, but I bet there's more. Also, do you think Joe's really mad, or is it bluster?" asked Colin.

"I just talked to him that once. I'd guess that he's okay. Them what's in charge of an investigation, likes to retain that position and be the decision maker," stated Ray with an opinion based upon his investigatory history.

"Oh, Glenn said too that there was no hit on fingerprints and there's no other distinguishing marks on John Doe. No missing young men from the Hispanic community in Dunkirk either, but then there's that white butt, so we shouldn't just check for MIA Hispanics. Lastly, Joe will be here on Thursday, early."

"That gives us two days, dos dias, on our own. Let's try not to screw things up too badly," said Ray. "Oh oh, Bill Morris is just down the street, coming for me. Gotta go. Sally's coming later for a check of skills and equipment. See ya."

"You can distinguish his car blocks away? You can tell it's Bill's car?" asked Colin.

Colin stood. Ray was at the curb. Bill's car stopped and he was out the driver's door, at the front passenger's door and settling his precious cargo, as he would any passenger.

Ray's window silently opened electrically and he said, "Thanks for the vote of confidence Colin, but Bill said he'd call when he got down in The Springs and my phone vibrated in my pocket. I am an amazing man, filled with many skills, but I'm still waiting for my extrasensory powers to kick in. Let yourself out."

CHAPTER 22

Colin kept himself busy as he performed all those seasonal outdoor chores that he often and repeatedly accomplished during any given summer. Those just planted hanging pots needed constant watering, or did it just seem that he was forever watering them? The lawn, enough said. Colin chose to organize his Amish shed. The shed was made at an Amish sawmill in Hartfield by Amish carpenters and their sons. It was a great shed, but all that classified it as being Amish was that it was made by Amish workers. It held a small work bench and tools, sporting equipment, folding things (chairs, ladders, tables), paper products, yard tools, paint and wood scraps all neatly stored, easily accessible. Having all those items on hand over the 4th picnic/reunion days would be an advantage. "Work well done has its own rewards", thought Colin as he completed the finer points of shed organization.

Lots of things that needed a thorough thought session were shuffled to the back of Colin's head. By ten o'clock, bursting with thoughts and thoughts about thinking, Colin was in his thinking spot. Once again, Colin knew that this spot, this highly personal piece of the Earth was important to his mental well-being and so, he thought.

Colin's first thought was concerned with how terrific it was to have Ray as a daily force in his life. Colin never expected to return to those "days of yesteryear". Over the years he had thought of Ray and was mad with himself for not making greater attempts to keep that relationship alive, but they each had places to go and people to see, all leading them forward to this halcyon summer. He'd be sure to enjoy these days. No amount of thinking could concoct the future.

As kids, Ray and Colin had gone to camp at some church property on the lake and now, maybe, the return to the lake would bring them some measured calm. A neighbor who wrote a book about living by the lake, any lake, said that the proximity to water was sure to provide a restorative state of mind that soothed in times of emotional unrest. Colin thought that that was so.

Colin thought too about something that wasn't as personal. The cadaver that Glenn Fourtney had taken a total second look at still hadn't been forthcoming with useful information. Age, height, general health and cause of death were just about all John Doe had been willing to share, but Colin wanted murderer information, not cadaver statistics. Just because there were young men, perhaps Hispanic men, renting in The Springs and the cadaver was perhaps a Hispanic man, that didn't mean that there was a connection. How could Colin, not Colin with the help of Ray or the machine of the sheriff's office, find that connection if it did indeed exist? As per his practice, thinking led Colin to do things that he thought feasible and logical and obvious, but yet could turn or have the potential to turn, silly or unnecessary or possibly even dangerous. Thinking, a great tool and ever so helpful if a stringent timeframe were imposed, was a skill Colin possessed.

Was thinking a skill, or a tool or a crutch?

Now he was thinking and walking quickly. The thought that he needed an up-close-and-personal look at The Landing and/or the current tenants was guiding his actions.

Colin went into his newly organized shed and found his tool belt. He also found a claw hammer, his 10-in-1 screwdriver and a coffee can of nails. His plan was to, in a neighborly fashion, check all the nails on the porch, stairs, decks and docks belonging to Ben and Christine Strand. He could pull that off. He could hammer. He could look like a professional hammerer. He added a hat to his hammerer wardrobe and was ready to punch the time clock when the telephone rang. He was going to not answer, let the machine take the message, but the name 'V. O'Brien' came on the phone screen.

"Hi honey," Colin answered. "I was wondering when you'd call."

"Oh Colin, you saved us from a mess trying to get settled here. Doug was at the gate when we got here and he got in the car and drove us to the hidden, believe me we never would have found this hidden, parking lot for the Sunrise Condo dwellers. An elevator took us to Aunt Jessie's apartment and, this is my favorite part, Yanita was there making beds and cleaning. It's a service, a freebee service, available and, here's my second favorite part, she'll be here tomorrow too. My least favorite part is that she does not cook for us. She's sweet, has some English and is from San Something. I'll get more information later. Anyway, thank you hon for making this work. Amy was all apology and I told her to forget it."

"I know how Doug operates. You've seen his yard and deck and boat and I was sure of his organizational skills and that he'd be able to make that all work," said Colin. "Is the place lovely?"

Vonny gave Colin more description and exuberance than he required, but Colin was happy with her happy. She said that they had been to the pool and were headed back after a bit of lunch. She promised to call back later. She wanted to get a daily schedule to see what and who was appearing and she'd call with details before dinner.

"Will you be home then? What are you doing for dinner? How's Ray? Heard from Ronny and Dan? Enough. Bye for now. Love ya! Love ya even more when I'm not with ya! Love ya even more when I'm not gonna be with ya for two or three days."

Before hanging up, Colin proclaimed his love for Vonny and assured her that he would hardly be able to cope with her in absentia. He could hear her spirited laughter as she hung up. How could she not laugh?

Colin, in his hammerer disguise, went straight to work. He started at the dock, but didn't stay there long because no one was there and there were no clothes, shoes or towels awaiting a swimmer's return. No one was at the community dock either. Probably everyone was home for lunch or out to lunch. Most boat slips and hoists were empty. It was a perfect day at the lake, albeit a Tuesday. No one cares what day it is when it's a lake day.

Colin had exhibited his hammering skills at the Strand dock, but soon packed up his gear and was off to perform act two of his highly authentic portrayal on the porch at Strand's Landing. The Landing was, or looked to be, devoid of tenants. Colin got into character and pounded in those errant nails that dared to sneak their heads above the wood that offered their assigned location. There were more errant nails than Colin thought there would be, but he was soon into character and presenting a credible performance. His pounding on the front steps, produced no attention from inside the cottage. He was fairly sure no one was inside, even late sleepers, so he moved up onto the porch and even, boldly, moved furniture to better facilitate his work output. He was by the door, furtively peaking in, by the windows, more furtive movement, and still no one emerged to inquire about his functioning.

Oh, what the heck, thought Colin. He opened the screen door, propped it open with a porch chair and he tried the door handle, not locked, and he turned it, pushed the door open and was quickly on his knees hammering onto the porch while his body was mostly inside. During this quick, slick move, Colin knocked over the Maxwell House nails and he then spent time picking them up, but mostly looking over the porch from his vantage point and checking to see if there was any traffic, vehicle or person, on the street. All clear, he thought, and in an instant he was up, turned around and into the living room frantically, well almost frantically, looking round, not touching or prying or opening or sorting. Nothing remarkable: not as sloppy as it might have been, dark because the curtains were drawn. Colin had seen worse, lived in worse; scattered videos, newspapers, magazines, empties, food containers, storage tubs of shoes, clothes, renegade pillows provided décor in this very casual setting.

He'd heard that muffler before. Last night... girl driver, late, interior light. A second, or was it third, slick, quick move got him out the door, it got closed, chair moved, screen door slammed, nails grabbed, to the stairs, to the ground, walking away toward the lake, the muffler sounding, but not in sight. No panic, just walk, stop at another porch and provide an encore performance.

CHAPTER 23

"You dork!" growled Ray. "You called my attempt at information seeking 'solidly surreptitious'. I believe that was the phrase you used. What do you call what you did? Commando Raiding 101," Ray continued. "I'd call your shenanigans a tour de farce."

Ray, on a dime, took a turn for the better. "I never coulda pulled that off. Colin, for an old, retired schoolmarm, ya done good. What'd ya learn? You had better talk."

Bill Morris had just dropped Ray off at Colin's front porch and was now sailing away up the street.

"Bill has sick, rich old ladies to take to the doctor in Westfield in his limo, so I got out here," said Ray trying to be nonchalant. "Did Sally show yet?"

"No Sally. She'll call to reschedule."

"Okay, Okay. Start again. Give me details. Come on!" said Ray.

"I was thinking about those guys at Strands. Here's what I did," started Colin. He told Ray about his disguise, better than pretending to be a pathetic old blind man, and about his hammering persona. Then he told how he stealthily created the opportunity to peruse the living room at the perp's house.

After semi-berating Colin for working outside the strict boundaries placed upon them by Sheriff Joe, Ray asked,

"Well, what did you learn?"

Colin hadn't thought about what he learned, he was just glad that he did not get caught.

"Well, what do you think I learned?" asked Colin. Turnabout is fair play.

"Tell me about the videos, newspapers, magazines, food boxes. What'd they call out to you?"

Colin had to absorb the question and then come up with an answer. Thank goodness he had all that thinking practice earlier this morning.

"'American' is what they called out," Colin finally blurted out. "They yelled 'young' too. Junk food. Junk movies. I don't get it. Don't get it at all."

There were a few moments of silence, time for Colin to get a seltzer water for himself and Ray.

"Fake, fake, fake, fake, fake," said Ray. "Do you remember that *Seinfeld* episode where Elaine tells Jerry that she was 'faking it' with him and she enumerated on all the 'fake' moments between them? Well these guys, whether two, three or four of them, whether there's tall folk or shortys, whether they are Hispanic or only partially Hispanic, remember they are from the white butt tribe of Hispanics, we really don't know much for sure about them. They're all fake, fake, fake, fake, fake. Lots of pretense, lots of sneakiness. Do you think that Mr. Strand might be able to get us info or have his lawyer friend call us, or better still call Joe?"

"Hang on Ray. We gotta think here. I know you have

B-more cop experience to fall back on, but 'round here weans like ta mosey on through our garden of information afore we pluck the fruits and flowers that are the ripest. D'ya know what um tryin' ta tell ya?"

"I don't know if I'm getting the exact message that you're sending out, Colin, but you're sounding like you're right outa *Mayberry RFD* and that you have lost your ever lovin', pea pickin' mind."

"Sorry Ray. I was still in my hammering disguise and slipped into a character from which it becomes difficult to separate oneself. You need to slap me on both cheeks and say 'snap out of it' and I will in turn say 'thanks, I needed that'. Are you up for that piece of drama?"

Colin's slapping suggestion brought both Ray and him to laughter and ignited talk about times-gone-by where they had adopted characters and carried on even in supermarkets and in front of company. They were never malicious or foul, but their "fun" was silly, offensive, loutish, irreverent and crude. Bodily noises, animal sounds and slapstickieness were always part of the drama.

The O'Brien phone rang. "Colin, it's the phone. Ya hear that, my extrasensory powers are kicking in. Bet it's Vonny," said Ray.

"Hi honey. What cha doin'?" said Vonny from far-off Chautauqua Institution.

"Ray and I were just reminiscing and getting ready to practice for the 4th. What are you and Amy up to this evening?"

"We are going for a gourmet pizza at a little shop on the grounds and then take a walk, have a cone and sit on our balcony and listen to the Chautauqua Symphony. This is the life in case I haven't mentioned it. First things first, sit down, put the phone on speaker and listen. Ready? Hi Ray. You two, just listen, you can ask any questions you'd like after I tell you what's happening at this side of the lake with regard to the Hispanic community. Ready? So, I was out on the balcony, we are up four floors, not too high, I can stand at the railing and not get nauseous. You can see the new Amphitheatre and lots of green space and over the trees to the lake and across the lake, I can see the Midway Roller Rink amid trees. I digress. I can see people walking around by the Amp. There's not a lot of walkers. Oh there are walkers for a lot of the seniors, but not walkers, people out getting exercise. Most people look like they have a destination and they are coolly dressed and clearly headed to that particular place. Down there among those walkers were two young Hispanic men. Yes, I think it's the Strand tenants. Honest. They are in t-shirts and shorts, flip flops and shades. And, these guys, I watched them for a while, are strolling. They've gone around the Amp four or five times. Questions?"

"Are you sure it is them? Come on! Bet they haven't got the gate fee. Wait, daddy has mucho pesos. Why are you so sure it's them?" asked Colin. Ray sat quietly.

After a few seconds, Vonny responded to Colin. "I followed them."

"What?" came the loud, incredulous response from both Colin and Ray.

"You're kidding. This is no joke, right?" continued Ray.

"No kidding. Amy was napping. I put on my shades, borrowed a huge straw hat from Aunt Jessie's hat tree and took a safe, leisurely walk around the Bestor Plaza and then back to the Amp and then down to the waterfront and then I followed them until they got on a jitney that was going to take them to the Main Gate. They had no idea who I was or if I was following them. You forget I am a mother of three, my following and observational skills are still intact."

Ray interrupted, "Vonny, it sounds like you did good, but don't do that again. Promise me. Let me come over and follow them around. Wait, no that won't work. One of them and I got up close and personal last night, he'd recognize me."

"What?" rejoined Vonny.

Ray, obviously not relying on professional protocols from his past, informed Vonny about his midnight encounter with The Landing tenant and while he was in cop zone, he told on Colin. Ray gave Colin street creds for his "perp turf invasion" and he downplayed any danger that Vonny might have thought existed.

"So," said Ray. "As the temporary senior officer on the case, I commend us all, but I also have to say that we should call Joe, Sheriff Joe. It's really his case, his force, his county and here we are playing cops and robbers. Remember Colin how we always did that as kids? We gotta stop.

"Vonny, I have one last question then you can go back to 'vacay mode'. What did you learn from your close encounter of the Hispanic kind? I told you what we know based upon our actions. Carefully review your observations and tell me what did you learn about these guys?"

Colin and Ray switched into chairs on the porch that were in the late afternoon shade.

"They are either very serious or scared," said Vonny. "Certainly not in as you call it 'vacay mode'. They were measuring things. No, there was no tape, no string run from tree to tree, but obviously, to me anyway, they were counting seats in the Amp, parking places by the Amp and time traveling from the Amp to the waterfront. This is the first year for this new Amp, forty million went into it over the winter. It has all the bells and whistles and sound equipment and cameras. Anyway, they stood by an Amp gate and watched as it emptied after a lecture. One was on one side of the Amp and the other was in the far back. I only knew he was back there when I saw his white t-shirt. He was almost hidden by bushes. I learned something else too. They've no time for girls. They are rather good looking young men and there are lots of good looking young ladies here too, staff and guests, but the boys weren't ogling, is that still a word?"

Vonny hardly took a breath, "New topic. Ready or not.
You know how each week has a theme here, some loose
topic umbrella that they can program under. Amy and I
are here for 'The Urban Garden, Arugula to Quinoa'. Seriously. But the good news is that the main stage performers
tomorrow night are 'The Red Hot Chili Peppers'. I don't
think they'll be giving gardening or cooking hints. Sorry. I
digressed. Are you two still there?"

After grunts of yes and yes dear, Vonny completed her
thoughts. "Next week is entitled 'South America, Social
Change and Its Future'. I'll let that sink in for a moment.

"Amy's up. I will call in the morning and give you more
details about that week or you could go on line and see
Chautauqua schedules and blurbs about upcoming speakers
and entertainment. I think they are headlining 'The Miami
Sound Machine' with what's-her-name. Bye."

CHAPTER 24

It wasn't long before Ray had CHQ.com on his computer screen.

"I will turn off the 'screen to sound' piece of this thing," said Ray. "I've been told that it's annoying. You can read to me."

"Absolutely not," replied Colin. "If you can stand me talking to the screen, I can deal with a screen talking to me. Vonny says I talk to the computer. Could be."

They spent the better half of an hour, side by side on kitchen chairs, at the computer and navigating the CHQ. com options. Colin later told Ray that it was like when they were kids and spent hours on a rolling hassock at Colin's house watching Hopalong Cassidy and Sky King and, of course, The Lone Arranger and Tonto. Now their screen time had more importance.

"That's enough," said Ray. "We don't want to get out of Week Two programming. Week Three is 'The Playwright as Social Critic' and I doubt that that is a draw for young men of pseudo-Hispanic persuasion. I'm forwarding this site to you, so go home and print off the daily schedule for all next week. You can do that, can't you? And come back with seltzer water, leftover cookies and an appetite. I'm putting an easy egg-plant casserole in the micro…it's in a Styrofoam server, just needs warming. We have to dissect that schedule. Move it," he concluded.

"You're just as bossy as you were when we were kids. I'm moving as quickly or as slowly as I decide to move. I'll be back when I am good and ready to be here," said Colin, the last few words given at the front door with his back to Ray.

As he slowly walked home, Colin realized that his dramatic, childish exeunt was probably lost on Ray, who was probably just intent upon getting dinner into the microwave.

As Colin entered his house by the kitchen door, the phone was ringing.

"Hello," answered Colin.

"Is Colly Wolly upsety wety?" came a sing-songy voice followed by a quick click initiated by the offending caller.

Dinner was great. Colin avoided his clever use of the word les aubergines and the conversation ricocheted all over the place. It was as though the nephew and the uncle hadn't experienced a twenty year separation. It was as though the twenty year separation had been the perfect catalyst for this perfect reunion. How can you have the reunion without the separation?

"The last thing I'll say about Gertrude Krutnot, 3rd grade teacher, 10th Street Elementary School was that she was hot for you. You got to be Hiawatha, and your girlfriend Clementine Shallock was Nokomis, daughter of the moon Nokomis, and I was the announcer. 'We are proud to present our interpretation of *Hiawatha* by Henry Wordsworth-or-whateverworth Longfellow,'" said Colin in high dudgeon mocking. "Gertrude and Raymond sitting in a tree k-i-s-s-i-n-g."

"Colin, that was over fifty years ago, and you are still bitter," replied Ray. "Truth is, Gertrude and Mr. Kyle Packer, 5th grade, were an item. I caught them in the cloak room once. That's why I was Hiawatha. Let it go, Colin. For the sake of humanity, let it go.

"Let's look at CHQ.com, Week Two. But before we even think of conflating the boys and Week Two…" said Ray and he was quickly interrupted by Colin.

"Hold the word. Conflating? Really?" said Colin.

"Yes. It's when two seemingly different items or topics blend or form a fusion and then move on as one. Got it."

"Confluence is the word you're looking for. That's the word that implies that the moving ahead together is logical and inevitable; the new entity has been formed by necessity and ultimately flows onward," was Colin's teacherly reply.

"Is this an English symposium or are we trying to draft a trajectory for the behavior of these boys? Either word works," said Ray. "As I was saying, if I may go on, is that we need to be sure that the boys and the week are running side-by-side and that they might soon join in a confluence of conflagrations."

Silence permeated the room. Ray put dishes in the sink. Colin put leftovers in the refrigerator. Then they each took a seat on the cushy way-overstuffed furniture in the living room. Colin sat making sure he could see out of the door.

"There is a high possibility that the boys and the week will intersect and move forward. We have to call Joe," said Ray's assessing the current situation.

"Hold on! I partially agree with you," said Colin. "It's the calling Joe part that I am unsure of. Just listen! We are trying to put non-Hispanics into the middle of a fiesta of Hispanic culture. And it looks like we are assigning nefarious plans to them. Start your thinking with Ben in Florida, move to Whitey, Vonny on the grounds, our interactions, Binky's encounters, Glenn Fourtney and Joe trying to make sense of dispirit pieces of information...don't forget white butts...I think we gotta just plain think."

Silence permeated the room. Colin moved to the small round table in the dining room section of the huge living room that constituted most of the downstairs floor plan. He spread out the sheets that his printer had produced and he called Ray over to join in the sorting process that he envisioned.

"Okay, we have five days of cultural activities to sort. First, we have to identify a supposed assignment for the boys. We do agree that they are interested in Chautauqua and that there is a draw of some kind for them. It's a

Hispanic draw although they are not actually Hispanic. Agreed?" asked Colin who was enjoying this problem solving activity much as he had done when he taught special education. Then, in school, the problems were clear… swearing in the cafeteria, kicked off the school bus, incomplete or nonexistent homework assignments…but now, in The Springs, years later, it wasn't so easy to assign intent.

"They hate someone, were sent to cause trouble, are waiting their turn to disrupt, to cause mayhem," blurted out Ray. "But then you can't go by me. I'm always looking for the bad guy, looking to prevent things actually. A person, a cause, a point of view…something is calling them to a confluence in the near, Week Two, future."

CHAPTER 25

"It's late, Ray. You must be beat. Let's call it a night. We have all day tomorrow since Joe's not here till Thursday…do not call him…we can continue this tomorrow. Ray?"

"There's something that we are missing," said Ray. "Can't figure if it's in the personalities or activities of Week Dos or if we should be concentrating on the boys. Just let me ramble. Is the swimming a cover? Are the boys as they say they are and the tans are part of the family's witness protection program? Are they on the Chautauqua grounds because they are casing the joint or are they feeling lonely for mommacita? Let's call Mr. Strand. He's has to be able to give us something. We're going to give him nothing. Let's do speaker phone. You introduce me and tell him that you are worried for my safety. Can we trust the boys? Where are they from? What does he want to know about how they are doing? Is he still in touch with the family or their lawyer? Etc. Etc.

"Thanks for letting me ramble. My team in Baltimore hated whenever I did that. Personally, I felt that it was constructive and gave them lots to think about and act upon. I'm not asking for your input. I am sure that your mouth is open and that you are ready to talk…and put away that tongue!"

Ben Strand answered his cell phone after the first ring.

"Colin, I am so happy to take the time away from my father-of-the-bride duties, which consists mostly of writing checks. I am glad to talk to you and your Uncle. Ray is it? Sorry that I won't get to talk with you in person, but I'm sure Colin and Vonny (what does she see in him?) will be your gracious guides in The Springs. What's up Colin? The Landing is still there, in one piece, I hope."

"Well Ben," began Colin. "We were just wondering if you can give us a bit of info on the boys so that we can interact better. We don't really see them much. I guess, the first thing we are wondering about is where are they from? Can you give us any family info? Truth is, it's South American week on the Chautauqua grounds and we can take them to something that might be of interest, but I'd hate to start an international incident if I somehow mix up cultures and political goals. What'd ya know that you can share?"

"They really do seem to be ignoring us all. And you know how friendly Maple Springers are," added Ray.

"Well, I must say you guys are being good sports up there. I did see the guy, the lawyer, that got me to rent to the guys up there now and he was surprised that the boys were still there. Turns out that this family wasn't a client of his, but had just moved into the development he lives in. The family recently went home to Panama. They went to a city near where Panama shares a border with Columbia. I think it was vacation or a wedding or funeral, not to stay, but they haven't returned yet. I think she was German, he was Columbian and the kids somewhere in between. He's an industrialist. I'm not sure what that means, but I do know that there are a lot of contractual issues involved with trading between countries. There are also a lot of shipping restrictions, and governmental oversight rears its ugly head too. They were here waiting for things to settle down at home…revolution, election fraud, voter unrest, who knows. I've had Cuban clients in similar situations, and believe me returning to the 'scene of the crime', so-to-speak, is a very difficult maneuver to pull off.

"Swimming, yes, I should mention that. Kaitlin said that Ronny told her, on Facebook I think, that she saw the boys and they were hardly Olympic swim material. Kaitlin thought she had seen them at a pool at a country club down here and she said that they were goof balls. Are they swimming up there? Their story about swimming and the Olympics is what helped to sway me into renting to them. Again, what's with that?"

"Well, they are out in the lake a lot and the lake is still cold. Binky sees them all the time. And speaking of Binky, she says that there are more than two guys. She's seen a variety of sizes and heights. If there is more than two, is that a lease breaker for you?" asked Ray.

"Truth be told again, there seems to be more than two when we consider the noise level," added Colin.

"This is sounding like a nightmare. We have so much

on our plate, our $49.99 a dinner plate to be exact if you ask Mr. Albert, our wedding consultant (a bargain he says) and now this," moaned Ben.

"Ben, Ben relax. We have this Maple Springs location of your vast estates under control. We are working to make the boys' stay comfortable and we want to be neighborly. Mi casa es su casa. Don't let this call get your bowels in an uproar," said Ray.

A good laugh was had by all and soon the call ended with Ben agreeing to stop worrying and to go get himself a scotch and soda. He also agreed to put the Hispanic boys homesteading at his Landing out of his mind.

"Whose idea was it to call him? I think we just doubled the size of any ulcer that he thought he had under control. But we did learn things. Colin, what did you learn?"

"I learned that they inherited their white butt from their Germanic mommacita. Maybe it was advantageous to tan and to look more Hispanic when they were in Florida or doing business or traveling in the Southern Hemisphere. I learned that swimming is their entree, but not really their be-all. Once I had a student that knew everything about baseball. He had a head for stats, remembered everything. But that was all that was in his head. He'd wow you with stats and you'd be impressed and then you gave him lots of slack for all that he couldn't, wouldn't do. I wonder where he is today. Anyway, these muchachos aren't here for swim-ming, but they are here with plans of some sort. What those plans are I don't know. Now you tell me what you learned from Ben Strand," prodded Colin.

"I learned that $49.99 a plate might break the Strand bank and that Mr. Albert could end up with a black-eye. I hope Kaitlin is a sweet thing that appreciates her father's love," said Ray. "I learned that the Hispanic family is off into the void. We had missing people all the time in Maryland. They just sort of faded away. Perhaps too, these boys aren't brothers. The parents are gone, possibly in hiding, and the boys, not necessarily biologically theirs, are on a mission. Aren't there sisters in California? I seem to remember you telling me that or was that info from some other case? I also learned that Ben does not really know the lawyer in Florida. That lawyer was just fishing for a friend and Ben took the bait, and we got the boys."

CHAPTER 26

Colin and Ray did cease investigatory activities late last night. They determined that they would be fresher in the morning. They thought they'd be more open to outside-of-the- box ideas about the boys and about their reasons for being north, in Maple Springs and on the Chautauqua grounds.

In the morning when Colin and Ray got back together, they picked right up where they had left off at the dining room table with Week Two spread out before them.

"The website lists the activities by day and time," said Colin. "They've listed Amphitheater Lectures, Amphitheatre Performances and The Arts. Actually there is overlap on all this stuff; sometimes the lecture is in the Amp and often the arts are performing arts scheduled in the Amp too. Plus there are other sites on the grounds where all this culture can happen. I'm overwhelmed just looking at the schedule. Wait though! Vonny saw them at the Amp, so let's start looking at the presentations there. The boys want to see someone, boo someone, disrupt, shoot…"

"Hang on my friend. You just said 'shoot'. Are you talking gun 'shoot'? How'd you jump there? What trick is your pea brain pulling on you?" said Ray. He wasn't scolding, perhaps he was on the verge of saying 'shoot' too, but he knew that he had to get in sync with Colin.

"Shoot is just part of a list I'm making. I could have said 'rob' or 'hold hostage' or 'heckle'. We are brainstorming here, throwing out ideas, stirring up the pot. Isn't this part of your B-Mo M O?"

"Leave shoot on the list. Read me the speakers on the Amp stage, not necessarily the performers," said Ray.

"Okay, I will try to be forthcoming and to not be censoring the information that is supplied by Chautauqua. Monday morning; Father Fredwardo Castaign from Argentina talking about Pope Francis; "A South American Prelate Sets Out to Change the World". In the afternoon a children's choir from Mexico will perform South American songs and dances. They perform each afternoon this whole week. The evening act is Melisando Cortado singing Bossa Nova music. On to Tuesday. Stop me if you think that something or someone could be in trouble.

"Tuesday morning: Carlos Vega-Mundono, a former prosecutor from the Brazilian Supreme Court has a talk entitled "The South American Shame; Human Trafficking"...Q & A to follow. The choir again and at night, the National Symphony Orchestra of Cuba, in the USA on a 20 city tour, will feature work by South American composers." Colin paused for a minute.

"Bingo, I thinko!" said Ray. "I guess the words 'prosecutor' and 'Cuba' are pinging in my head. The South American Shame, that's actually written there? Human Trafficking? This guy Carlos is gonna roll out a continent's shame for the whole world to see? And Cuba, that revolution will never be completely over. Here's something else to think about too, 'political asylum'. Perhaps an orchestra member or members are going to seek asylum and our boys are assisting. They are on a twenty city tour you said. This might be the easiest place to slip away from the orchestra and then hide out in Maple Springs and apply for political asylum. Stop me anytime you think I'm losing it."

"You're brainstorming, Ray," said Colin. "It's okay. I'm going to move on to Wednesday.

"The morning's speaker is Guido Guayasamin, great-grandson of Oswaldo Guayasamin, who is said to be the greatest master painter and sculptor to be born in South America. The grandson's speech is entitled 'Growing up with Greatness'. It says here too that 18 of Guayasamin's most famous paintings are to be on display in the Chautauqua Gallery, the first such exhibit outside of the Southern Hemisphere. Again with the choir in the Amp and then at night there is a concert version of the opera *Carmen* on the Amp stage with the full Chautauqua Symphony Orchestra, Metropolitan Opera voices and it's to be sung in Spanish.

"No bells going off?" asked Colin.

"Art works," said Ray. "Did you know that stealing art and fencing it to rich folk is the most prevalent of all crimes of theft, even more common and profitable than stealing arms and jewels. Could an art heist be in the offing? Those paintings could be worth millions, tens of millions. Maybe your friend Doug can tell you about gallery security."

"On to Thursday...that choir is up for the fourth time and there is a panel on the Amp stage in the morning to discuss 'Can South American Cinema break into the World of Film?' and the three people presenting are all South American film directors who have had Hollywood successes. In the afternoon and then again at night there is a theatrical production in Norton Hall of *The Motorcycle Diaries* based upon the writings of Che Guevara written by South American playwright Carlos Carlos Rivero. Nothing on the Amp stage at night."

"Colin, are we out in La La Land somewhere? Is this a wild goose chase? We have non-Hispanics that we are trying to put into Hispanic and pseudo-Hispanic pigeon holes. As I said earlier, are we trying to make sense out of the nonsensical?" asked Ray.

"Let's lay out Friday and then try to bring it all together. Here's Friday: that choir, Amp morning speaker talking about 'Hemmingway's Cuban Influences' and later a documentary entitled *Papa Loves Cuba* will be presented at an indoor hall. 'The Miami Sound Machine featuring Gloria Estefan' is on the Amp stage at night and in the afternoon at Norton Hall, there is a panel discussion entitled 'Our Continent and the Dictators Who Savaged Our Humanity'. Bingo! I had to chime in before you. Bingo or no bingo or big bingo, what say you?"

"Big bingo works for me," chimed in Ray. "But wait.

Look what we're doing. There is no logic to what we are doing. Again, there's something missing. It's like we're desperate for a perp or a crime or a situation to prevent. And, we found possible perps. Now we are looking for their possible crime so that we can possibly prevent what probably won't happen. Sounds logical, doesn't it? But this is not the way to proceed with an investigation.

"It's time for a list. I always made pro/con lists and using that listing technique to highlight information and evidence was always helpful," said Ray.

"I like it," said Colin. "I'd say that we should make two lists based upon the five days of Week Two that we just reviewed: list #1. the situations or people that are just sitting there inciting an 'interaction with dissent' and; list # 2. the possible acts of dissention that could emerge," concluded Colin.

"I love it. This will focus us. Speak oh wise one," responded Ray.

Colin and Ray worked without distraction to create the lists that Ray proposed that they thought that they so desperately needed:

List # 1 *Possible Inciting Forces or People*
Prosecutor
SA shame/human trafficking
Political asylum/musicians
Cuba (band, 'Papa')
Art theft (18 paintings)
Speakers re dictators

List #2 <u>Possible Acts of Dissent</u>
Booing/Heckling
Disruption/large scale
Violence/ shooting/etc.
Robbery (art)
Hold hostage/kidnap
Seek asylum

"These lists help," said Colin, "but I think all they have done is to convince me that there is going to be an 'interaction with dissent'. We have the place, even the exact times on that Week Two calendar and we even think that we have perps. Just once more for my sake, tell me why the boys at The Landing have been labeled as perps."

This last interchange produced, to Ray's great joy, a list that was surely going to conflate possible perps with the already prepared list of 'Possible Inciting Forces or People' and 'Possible Acts of Dissent'.

List #3 <u>Why "the boys" qualify as "perps"</u>
Swimming is a "lie"
"Spanglish" (pseudo) Hispanic
Avoidance of Springers
Only two seen at a time
White butts/dyed hair
A cadaver … suspected violence/suspected associate

Suspect "back story" (family, FL, SA)
"casing" Chautauqua

Ray's cell phone rang and then announced, "V. O'Brien calling. V. O'Brien calling."

"I can't talk now. You-know-who is here. I'll call you back when you-know-who goes you- know-where," answered Ray.

"Hi Ray. I called Colin at home, got no answer and decided that I needed to talk to him and you, so that's why I called on your cell. What are you two doing? I hope you're finding time for Colin's music lessons."

"We are fine, relaxing and will soon get out the guitar. Here, I'll put this phone on speaker and we can all have a chat."

"Hi Honey, Vonny here with more insights into the wanderings of the Maple Springs Hispanic Duo. Ya wanna hear what happened today? You'll like it. Don't tell me you two are just sitting around and not playing deputy.

"Well?" said Vonny and she held her peace.

"Yes dear," said Colin. "Give us all the new details you have. Did you have breakfast with the guys? Are they on the balcony with you now? Did you invite them over for July 4th?"

"Let me just start. Stop me if you have questions. Do not stop me to scold me. So, this morning I was having coffee and I looked over the railing to see how busy the grounds were. With the holiday coming up, sometimes the place empties out a bit. Anyway, there they were, los muchachos, strolling the plaza. Guess what I did. You won't guess. Guess. Anyway, I got shades, a straw hat and went down stairs ASAP. Here's the best part. Aunt Jessie has one of those scooters, you know an electric three wheel thing. Her's is called a 'Golden Buzzaround'. It's easy to drive and all. Anyway, Amy showed me how to use it yesterday and I was sure that I wouldn't have to, but I thought that this would be a great disguise. Isn't that silly, a grown up resorting to a disguise. Anyway, I got the Buzzaround going and I followed the guys for quite a while. Always discrete. Always thinking of what I was learning. Aren't you proud? No need to answer that question just yet. Anyway, they stopped for coffee, talked with a young lady at the cafe and then went down to the waterfront. I stuck with them, but am determined to get back to that girl at the coffee shop. Proud of me yet? Anyway, at the shore the guys walked out on the community docks, looked up and down, tested the water, walked more, walked south actually, down the shore as far as they could, till they came to private land. I stayed way back, pretended sunning and looking at the water. When they returned, walking north to where they had started walking on the shoreline, I went ahead back to the plaza by the bookstore. I slowed down and they walked by me, so I was following them at their own doing. So, to end this long story, they sat on a park bench, the girl came out of the cafe and left with them. She looked familiar somehow. I bet she is how they got here. You know, I bet she brought them here this morning. So, I just parked my Buzzaround (I gotta get me one of those for The Springs) and I called you two. If that girl is taking them right home, they should be there soon. Now is the time to say 'good work Vonny, you are an asset to this team, that was ingenious following and so safe'. I would tell you what I learned about those guys, but I will save that for a call after supper and before the 'Chili Peppers'. Now get out there and look for the taxi bringing the boys home, get that license number, make, model, etc. Over and out."

"Looks like our mole on the Chautauqua grounds is on the job," said Ray. "Let's get outside and see if the young lady does indeed bring the boys home. I am going to sit on the front steps and practice chords on the guitar. You, Colin, need to get a vantage point out there on someone's lawn so that you see the license number and all those other things that Vonny brought to our attention. Be weeding or edging, something near the road. Get a good look at the girl. We will have to get the name of the coffee shop on the grounds too. Places! Don't come back here until the guys are home."

Soon, Ray was sitting and strumming. Colin hurried home and within minutes he was back with his bucket of gardening tools and a kneeler. He found a place on a lawn across the street and down one cottage from The Landing. The Maple Springs posse of two was in place and ready for action. In no time at all, Colin heard that same offending muffler that he had already heard twice in The Springs. The car rolled into place in front of The Landing and sat there sputtering while the boys got out. The car wasn't as decrepit as one would think that it would be if it were to be judged by its audio effect alone. Colin knew it was a Chevy, probably a 2013 or newer, dark blue, body intact. The plates indicated that its registration was New York State…MHH 1066 or as Colin repeated silently to himself, Minnie Ha Ha, Battle of Hastings. Colin couldn't get a good look at the driver; she was female and young and she appeared small behind the wheel of what appeared to be a big, four door car.

Colin continued his work around the base of a tree; he attacked the untrimmed grass and extricated a weed or two in the process. The car wasn't long on the street and the boys weren't long on the porch. As soon as the music started to float out of The Landing, Colin carefully and not hurriedly gathered his tools and walked to Ray's and sat on the steps.

"Well, Ray. That was, as I'm sure you heard, the same car that has been here before. I have the license number. It's a Chevy, a late model, dark blue. Joe can trace it. Before you ask, I learned nothing new about the boys and I really only got a glimpse of the girl driving. She was little, young, possibly a Latina," said Colin by way of concluding their brief investigatory stake-out.

"I learned that the car needs a ring job and that the muffler needs to be reattached. I think the muffler is serviceable, but it's rattling along under there. It's gonna be left behind at some point if the owner doesn't get it strapped back into place. Let's take the tandem for a ride and check out the lake front and see too if Claudia is at home. I know, I know, Binky," said Ray.

Colin placed his bucket of gardening tools and his kneeler on Ray's front porch and got the tandem from the enclosed back porch. When he returned with the bike, Ray was on his cell phone.

"Colin, it's our fearless leader, Sheriff Joe. He's on his way home early and he's by Olean on route 86 and should be here in an hour. He's asked what we've learned in the two days he's been gone. Here, you talk to him," said Ray as he placed the phone on the top porch step and quickly moved inside the house with his guitar in hand.

Great, thought Colin.

"Hi Joe. How was the seminar? Not much new here. I guess it'd be best if we three talked in person once you are back investigating. What's your plan," asked Colin.

"You tell me what my plan is," said Joe.

There was a moment for contemplating.

"Is there something that needs untangling?" asked Joe.

A second moment for contemplating was provided.

"I am answering my own questions," said Joe, "you're not. I am also putting on my siren for the next few miles. Sit tight. We'll talk."

CHAPTER 27

Within the hour there was what Joe referred to as a "meeting of the minds" at Ray McGill's house. Currently there were five minds that had assembled for the meeting. During the one hour from the time that Colin hung up from his phone call with Joe, off in Olean somewhere, until the moment that Joe walked in the front door at Ray's there had been a lot of scrambling on the parts of those in attendance.

"Thank you all for your attendance here on this lovely summer day on the shores of Lake Chautauqua. Vonny, I am surprised to see you, but you must have something you'd like to contribute or you'd be elsewhere having fun. When we start, we will start with you so that you can get on with whatever it is you need to do. Glenn, glad that you are joining us. I always find that you detail people help to cut to the chase when the theoretical folks are dithering around in a quagmire. And Ray and Colin, reluctant deputies that you are, I'm sure your input at this meeting will be significant," said Sheriff Joe Green in his capacity as convener, sheriff, decider and friend.

"Vonny, you know that we are interested in the movement of the tenants at Strand's. Tell us what you know."

Vonny began the meeting. "First I should tell you, a large sheet pizza from Coppola's will be here in an hour.

There's a cooler of pop and beer on the porch. I hope to be gone by then, but enjoy. I am staying with a friend in a condo with a pool, etc. on the grounds of the Institution and I am returning to see *The Red Hot Chili Peppers* in the Amp. Enough about me. While enjoying my balcony at my condo, I should mention too that they have a day spa, I saw our young Hispanic neighbors walking on the grounds, twice".

Vonny carefully told the other attendees about her two "encounters of the Hispanic kind" as she referred to the two instances whereby she, again her words, "stalked the perps" through the grounds. She particularly noted their interest in the waterfront and their "measuring" of the Amp area. She told too about the young lady at the café that the boys seemed to know.

"I've seen that young lady somewhere other than at the Institution. That's my story. Just me hanging around and them not knowing who I am, but it was weird too. Want to know what I think? They have a 'caper' that they are planning. 'Caper' is the wrong word, but you know what I mean. They were casing the joint. They have ulterior motives, probably not positive or PC or socially acceptable.

"I told Ray and Colin about both of these encounters and they told me about their trailing experiences, so between us three, I'd say that we kept an eye on the boys just as you asked Sheriff Joe. Can I go now? Those 'Chili Peppers' are calling my name and Amy my friend is next door waiting for me."

The four attending gentlemen rose to thank Vonny for her contribution to the meeting and to tell her to enjoy the rest of her evening, Colin got a kiss, and she was gone from the room.

"I wonder if the trailing experiences of Deputy O'Brien and Deputy McGill would have been a part of this confab had Vonny not so kindly informed us of their existence. Who would like to start?" asked Joe.

Colin, not shy, embarrassed or reticent at all, began. "First, here is the license number of the car belonging to the waitress at the Chautauqua café that Vonny referred to in her little speech here just a moment ago. That car has been here at least three times. The last time it brought the boys home. That was earlier today."

Colin gave Joe the paper that he had written the license number on and Joe gave it to Glenn who left the room with it.

Colin began afresh and managed to fill up a good twenty minutes regarding the information that he and Ray had acquired within the last two days. He also relayed details concerning Binky's observations at the lakefront. He was almost casual in telling the story about getting into the Strand's house as a repairman hammering errant nails back into place. He carefully told about each time he saw the boys at their house, at the waterfront, in a car. He also shared the three lists that he and Ray had made, each time giving ample credit to Ray for his part in their assemblage.

"But, and I am sure that you'll agree Joe," continued Colin, 'the best thing we did was to scan carefully Chautauqua's Week Two programming for possible instigators, possible people or situations that might be drawing the boys to the grounds. We, and correct me if you think I'm wrong Ray, we do not think that it is a coincidence that next week is South American week at the Institution. These guys, and probably their dead friend, are here directing a confluence of people, events and surroundings toward an end of negativity.

"Was that too much?" concluded Colin. "I got caught up in the moment."

Glenn returned to the room. "That was easy. The car belongs to the Pastor at St. Timothy's. According to the dispatcher, Matt, who attends St. Timothy's, the car was probably driven by Flora Sousa who is a Honduran student currently living with the Pastor. Flora, everyone calls her Flower, must have met the boys in Bemus and she offered to take them to the grounds. We need to talk to her and maybe even move her to someplace else for a few days. Matt said he'd call the parsonage and ask Flora to stay put. I'd say she's not involved in the 'caper' that Colin has envisioned. The boys might have said things that meant nothing to Flower, but to us that information might fit into the scenario we are trying to concoct."

"Thanks Glenn. While you've got the floor, do you have anything else to add to the autopsy information that we already have?" asked Joe. "Then you're on Ray. I'm not ignoring you."

"I appreciate all that you have said about the young men that are here in The Springs," said Glenn. "I can see easily how my guy, John Doe, was part of that crew. The tanning and the dyed hair, and let's not forget the white butt, all jibe. I had the swim coach at Fredonia come look at the body and he said that he did not think that the somatotype was that of a swimmer, but he said that anyone with any body type can for sure learn to swim and become proficient at it. This body however did not appear to the coach or me to be a body that had been in training for the role of champion swimmer."

"Thanks Glenn. Stick around. When we are finished here, I have other things to talk to you about," said Joe.

"I'm not leaving till after that pizza gets delivered," said Glenn.

"Okay Ray, you're up," said Joe as he moved to a chair closer to Ray that had been vacated by Vonny.

"Now I know how Colin felt when he was always picked last for teams when he was a kid," said Ray with a laugh.

"Colin relayed very clearly what happened around here in the recent past. He left for me to relate the details about my 'up close and personal' walk with one of the boys that time when I feigned that I was lost. Colin got in the house, but I was right there with the guy, hanging on. Before my accident I would never have taken a man's arm and pulled him in like that. I shook a hand here and there and might have wrestled or jostled a perp, but in-close work was out. To this day I still won't slow dance with a guy, but I think vibes and tensions are now easy for me to read. I will say that this guy was my size. I pulled him close when I took his arm and our shoulders were at the same level and this guy had a bad vibe, a tightness that said fear to me. I didn't see their size or their body type or their white butt, but I know a nervous and jerky would-be perp when I meet them up-close and personal."

Ray's heartfelt and highly personal remarks were understood and appreciated by the assembled professionals.

"There is still something we are missing," added Ray. "Either we are unwilling, don't have enough information or are quibbling. I love crossing t's and dotting i's, but at some time, and soon, we gotta make a move, use that pot or else. Today is shot, we have this tight, active weekend coming up and Week Two, 'South America, Social Change and its Future', looms."

"I smell pizza," said Joe. "The kid must have left it on the porch. Let's eat, I am starved, I had a Rueben in Binghamton at eleven o'clock. Then we will get right back in these chairs and finish this information gathering session. We will then map our immediate future plans. Immediate… I don't want you thinking that we are planning retirements and funerals. Let's eat."

CHAPTER 28

Thin crust, white pizza made with organic roasted vegetables enjoyed with a cold beer was the perfect break for the brain-trust of intense investigators sequestered at Ray's summer digs. Glenn and Ray, who had just met, hit it off just fine with talk of favorite professional sports teams and bluegrass music. Colin, with zero interest in both those areas of conversation listened intently and yet maintained his zero interest level. Joe was on the telephone during the forty-five minutes of supper break.

"Shannon and the kids are fine," said Joe. "I just spoke to them all. I made lots of promises. It will be a busy weekend.

"I called Matt too and Flower is going to stay with him and his wife and two kids. She's babysat there during the school year, she goes to JCC, so it's a good move. He talked to Flower and as we thought, she met the boys in Bemus and was just being friendly. Apparently they didn't talk much, but they did say that they would be leaving some time during next week. They said that their rental time was up."

"Sounds like a list in the offing," said Ray.

"I love it," said Glenn.

"I got paper and pen," said Colin.

"Okay, we give this one hour and then call it a night,"

said Joe. "I have a few clarifying question first. What is the title of this list? What are we listing? Are we brainstorming where anything goes, or must the list that is crying to be made be based upon facts? You remember facts, right? Are we compiling a list of facts leading to obvious conclusions that will guide us in the next moves in this case? Are we solving a murder? Preventing a future crime? Framing our Hispanic neighbors? I refuse to move ahead until we have a title for this list. Your turn. Anyone." Joe sat and began munching on the pizza crusts that he had previously left on his plate for future nibbling.

The list aficionados in the room sat silent.

Joe too was silent except for pizza crust nibbling sounds.

Finally, Joe spoke. "No new list. Let's return to List #3, so ably formed by Ray and Colin. Convince me, all of you, that los muchachos should be under suspicion."

"Let's start with the body found at the Marina at Long Point," said Glenn. "I always like to point out the obvious. We all agree that he actually was or could probably have been part of the gang at The Landing."

"No one ever saw him here for sure. Nothing to connect him with the other boys. There are lots of tanners and dyers out there. We haven't been able to identify him through prints or any other means," said Joe.

"But we do know, for sure, that he was murdered," said Glenn. "All the toxicology tests say drowning, and there's no body system that failed him before he hit the water; there was no heart business, no aneurism, no shut down of a body system and no blunt force blow to the head. Just the pesky evidence that he was held in an environment that was not conducive to the function of the human respiratory system."

"Cadaver is on our list. Is there another item to hash over? Colin? You coveted a list. You can keep us going. Next item," said Joe speaking directly to Colin in his leadership role.

"I'm going to bundle a couple items under one title," started Colin. "Guess the title is 'Lies' and the items under that title are 'Hispanic background' and 'Olympic swimmers', their past and their present. I guess it's not illegal to fake one's past, present and future, but it makes one look guilty. Add the cadaver and now their casing the joint on the Chautauqua grounds and considering the upcoming South American week and voila we have suspicious folks that we need to get in here to talk to."

"Time for a professional to jump in here," said Joe.

"I couldn't agree more," said Ray. "I think that...."

"There are two professionals in the room," interrupted Joe. "Both are currently charged with the safety of our Chautauqua County citizens and both are currently working in their assigned jurisdiction. Glenn and I are those two officers and we are not reticent to take charge here. Glenn, I will lead. You feel free to add to what I am saying and your agreement at the end will be most helpful and is required."

Glenn nodded his assent and probably his relief.

When Joe began talking again, the recent deputy desig-
nees kept quiet.

"Okay," said Joe. "I'm glad that we went back to List #3
and I think that there is enough there to convince us all that
the boys at The Landing are to be classified as suspects. I
am also convinced that the items on that list aren't defini-
tive enough to warrant a house call at The Landing. If these
pseudo-Hispanics are here for a 'caper', there could be other
co-conspirators around here somewhere. They could be
somewhere around the lake or on the Chautauqua grounds.
We don't know how many there are. Was John Doe involved with these guys? Why are they hiding out here in
The Springs? How many are here now? Why the Hispanic
disguises? If we show our hand, they'll abort their plans
and will probably skip town. And, believe me, they'll set up
shop elsewhere and attempt to complete the 'caper'.

"Let's talk about the Week Two schedule for a minute.
I daresay all those presenters, in the Amp and otherwise,
are each on a tour of some kind. The Cubano orchestra for
example is storming twenty cities. The eighteen very valuable art pieces are here for four weeks. But, we have to think
of the speakers and performers who will all be headed here
in busses and trucks to be part of the Chautauqua experience. We have to offer them a safe environment to come
into. There are many other constituents for us to consider
also: staffs of presenters, Chautauqua guests, employees,
businesses on the grounds, our local citizenry.

"So, as the leading professional lawman here, I say we look carefully at the Week Two schedule and project where and when the 'caper' is to be enacted. Knowing what could incite the 'caper' will lead us in knowing the form of dissent to be enacted. In other words, we have the actors and the setting and now we need to know the activity that will motivate our actors to perform their drama. Did I make myself clear?" said Sheriff Joe Green in a final and clear-as- can-be-manner as only he can manage on a regular basis.

CHAPTER 29

"Oh, I missed you honey," Colin said as he hugged Vonny. "But we were busy and I was so glad that you got to be relaxing. You put in some good time on the 'caper' with los muchachos too. Even Joe is using the word 'caper' now. It works. We have no idea what we are looking for so 'caper' fits. You directed the action to the grounds too. We are sure that the boys and the grounds equals 'caper'. Enough! What are you doing home again?"

"Colin, back to Joe and you guys in a minute, but first I'll answer your question. Amy and I were eating and then we suddenly realized that tomorrow would be July 3rd and right behind it was the 4th. You and I are having 35 people here for a reunion. We lost all track of days and we were off doing nothing and there is so much to do. You and I have one day to get our act together. Amy and I saw the first half of the *Chili Peppers* concert and then headed home. We beat the crowd leaving the grounds. The kids will be home tomorrow and then the hoards descend. And I promised pies. Ray's gang will be here tomorrow too…all I can think is food, towels, chairs, food, Wi-Fi, food. We can't possibly be ready," said Vonny with a panicked look on her face.

"Yes, we will get back to Joe and the 'caper', but sit, let me remind you of a few things." Vonny sat. "Remember, you got all the paper products last week. Ray and I ordered all the grill stuff from Vicki and she will be here tomorrow with other stuff too. I forgot all that we ordered. AND the family is bringing food and chairs, the weather forecast calls for sun and more sun for the next few days. The kayaks are all cleaned, the dock and fire pit at the shore are all set too. Remember too, Dianne won't be here and we can park in her drive and on her lawn and use her refrigerator. She has an icemaker in her garage too. We are all set, I'd say."

"Then, I'm headed back to Aunt Jessie's," said Vonny as she grabbed Colin and kissed him goodbye. "Kidding! Okay, if you say we are all set, I agree. If I made pies, I would have to make eight and I am not ready for that. Pies are overrated. The family isn't coming for pie or to inspect anyway. Right? Convince me of that, will ya."

"Can I tell you the plan that we concocted after you left this afternoon? Oh and thanks for the pizza. You are a sweetheart. The plan; thanks to you, we decided that the boys at The Landing are here for no good and the no good will take place on the grounds at Chautauqua during Week Two of programming. So here's what we have...we have four days before Week Two starts. We also have what we are calling instigators or motivators which are people, topics or causes being presented on the grounds that could be the fuel that ignites the dissenting action that the boys are plotting. We have a list of possible acts of civil disobedience that the boys could be contemplating, but we are concentrating on the targets, you know the motivators. Any questions?"

Vonny did have questions and Colin gave honest, straightforward answers. He told her about the "meeting of the minds" that had been adjourned earlier and how each of the men had a topic or a person or two to google and to be prepared to discuss when the minds met next on Saturday, July 5th, 3:30. He told her too that that plan had changed quickly.

"Ray was eager to do research," Colin continued. "You should see him at that computer keyboard. Then I had a brainstorm. I called Doug and invited him to Ray's house thinking that we could get Chautauqua security information from him. I sort of told him that there was a 'possible' dissenter that might cause a problem during Week Two and that I had some questions for him regarding programming and security. When he arrived at Ray's, he had with him, Susie Stein who is, wait for it, the Program Supervisor on the grounds for all nine weeks. She doesn't set the schedule, a committee does that, but she is the coordinator for housing, transportation, food and tech stuff once the performers and speakers get in house. She brought a laptop and knew everything about each person and each event that was to be part of Week Two.

"You will be proud of me, of what I did next. I called Joe. He came right back and after a bit, he confided in Doug and Susie about perps and 'capers' and acts of dissent. So, long story short, Susie and Ray and I went through the entire week and made a list of anyone or any event that could have what Susie described as having a 'hint of being internationally contaminated'. Susie says that the Institution doesn't avoid the subjects or people that stir the ire of the international community, but they pride themselves on thinking of safety and balance and civility. While we were gleaning the schedule, Joe and Doug talked security, Chautauqua's lockdown plan, how to get cars and firetrucks on the grounds, etc. Doug assured Joe that the fact that Chautauqua was a community surrounded by fences and walls and a waterfront was to the Institution's advantage. Doug assured Joe that security was always concern number one. Joe was worried particularly about the eighteen Guayasamin paintings in the gallery for four weeks; if the 'caper' was to be art theft, was Chautauqua prepared to fend off that possibility? Again, Doug assured Joe that a $200,000 alarm system had been installed at the gallery within the past two years and human guards would be in place 24/7. Little old lady volunteer docents would not be guarding the Guayasamin art work. Joe was convinced of the totality of the security on the grounds, but did a quick grimace when Doug told Joe that the eighteen pieces of art, paintings and sculptures, were valued at $24,000,000.

"This long story short is becoming a long story even longer, but just let me finish. Susie, Ray and I honed the list of possible 'caper' instigators to five events and/or people involved during Week Two. Here's the list:

Carlos Vega-Mundono... Brazilian prosecutor of

human traffickers in SA...Tuesday

Antonia Garza... Cuban orchestra director, constant critic of the Cuban government, accused of helping musician defectors...Tuesday

Benita Martino/Chava Dias/Tevo Tonita ... movie directors, all left SA under duress because of political content of their films...Thursday

A TBA panel of South Americans who are super critical of past dictators and their political parties who have 'savaged the humanity' of SA...Friday

Documentary producers presenting a work regarding Hemmingway and Cuba, but who have in the past produced documentaries highly critical of oil and lumbering companies who have 'pillaged the natural elements' of SA... Friday

"Susie says that if there is a target in the Week Two lineup that it would have to be one of these five situations. The others performers and presentations are not at all controversial and indeed most are of American, North American, origin; the opera, the choir, the play and the musicians are wrapped in tidy reputations.

"I told Susie that we knew relatives of the Ecuadorian artist, Guayasamin. She was sure that there would be no problem with that piece of the week. It was all arranged through the Ecuadorian Council in New York City. The grandson who is to speak lives in Columbia, she said. He is traveling here for the week. Susie thinks he is staying with local relatives. Must be Carmen. Can you call and verify all that with her. We should try to be there for the talk and the gallery opening too. Don't pass along any scary details. So far we are keeping all of this under wraps. See if Carmen has freebies would ya?"

Vonny was on the front porch obviously talking to the kids. She always called the kids when she knew they would be on the road, whether they were headed home or on a road trip elsewhere; "be sure you're rested, watch for speed signs, set your cruise, drive to conditions, see you soon, love you".

Colin sat in an Adirondack chair on the lawn next to the pavilion out back. He dialed Joe Green's private cell number but only got the answering machine.

"Hey Joe. It's Colin in The Springs. My mind is working overtime and I think I need to talk to you for a minute. Give me a call. I'll be up late, can't sleep."

The ringing of the cordless phone on Colin's lap woke him with a start. "Hello, who is this?" is all Colin could get out.

It was Sheriff Green. "Thought you couldn't sleep. You're sounding all garbly. What's up?"

"Hey Joe, thanks for calling. I'm feeling dumb about

what I'm going to say, but here goes. The Springs is filling up. Lots of the summer gang and their families are arriving this evening and tomorrow it'll be a zoo around here. We have a parade on the 4th and a community cocktail party and fun and games at the community dock. Oh and we have a house of pseudo-Hispanic bad-boys too. Did I overstate my concern?"

"Colin, Colin, Colin. You are right on task, a regular one-man neighborhood watch, a modern day Minuteman, McGruff incarnate. I fully understand your concern and I am one step ahead of you. It does seem like a long time till we reconvene on Saturday so listen carefully now. There isn't much to worry about. The boys may not even be hanging in the hood this weekend. Week Two, their reason for being here, doesn't start for four days. Let me explain your personal insurance policy. Vanessa and the Sheriff's Power Boat will be tied up at the community dock for the next three days. We'll have other boats cover the lake, but she'll be there being visible, helping boat owners and talking to kids and giving out those brochures about fireworks. I spoke to Binky and she will keep an eye on Vanessa and make sure she has food. AND, are you ready, two of our guys, you remember Pete Gianna and Steve Johnson, detectives, will be staying at Dianne Warren's right by you. I told them they could come to your 4th of July party. They'll just hang around, be at the lake, fish. Eileen is giving them a small boat to use. Los muchachos don't know we have them on our radar, so we are surveilling and simultaneously celebrating our nation's birthday…what a deal. So my friend, relax, enjoy your family. I may even show up. I'll wear my civvies of course.

"I am going to leave you with a conundrum that hasn't been addressed. Ready? Why are the boys presenting themselves as Hispanic? The fact that Week Two is wrapped around South America is what lured the boys here. Right? Why can't they be English speaking Caucasians? Just a thought. Ponder away." Joe hung up without a goodbye and Colin sat there looking at the phone until it started to produce that fast-paced dial tone that everyone finds so annoying.

By the time Colin and Vonny got into bed, all areas that were of concern to them were under control:

the kids had their travel instructions,

Doug and Susie Stein were conducting short, need-to-know meetings with Chautauqua Institution security and hospitality folks,

there was a solid plan to insure that The Springs was 4th of July ready and safe,

the O'Brien/McGill/Jackson Family Reunion was in standby mode and would, when appropriate, erupt into a full-bodied extravaganza including food coordination by Vicki and Vonny's take-charge mom,

the special guests from Baltimore had been briefed by Ray,

Los muchachos were on their own for the next three days.

CHAPTER 30

"The best-laid plans of mice and men often go awry"....but in the case where Joe Green and Colin O'Brien were planning for the 4th of July weekend at Maple Springs, while simultaneously keeping tabs on suspects laying low in the same Springs, those plans were going well.

Things moved forward in all areas in nice trajectories with plans coming to fruition and people and plans being embraced appropriately...all was ready, then transpired and yielded more than acceptable results. The Family Reunion was wonderful in every way. It was a true reunion. The fabled Maple Springs events, led by the grandchildren of those who initiated the events years earlier, were a huge success. Safety, thankfully, took precedence.

On July 3rd instead of making pies, Vonny spent the day hugging arrivees and introducing friends, neighbors, and family in the effort to make everyone comfortable and open to joining in with games, meals, songs and chores. The assembled turned out to be a congenial group peaked for fun, family and food. And fun, family and food it was for most of the 3rd and all of the 4th and till about noon on the 5th when some of the attendees had to leave and those that stayed were intent on chillin'. The majority of family members in attendance for the reunion were day-trippers and they reluctantly headed home after the profusion of

Midway State Park fireworks reached its noisy, colorful and all-round spectacular end.

On Saturday the 5th, after the raucous 4th, The Springs retired to its laid-back self as the visitors headed home. The O'Brien children and their mates were visiting with Jamestown friends and were not expected home for dinner. The Baltimore contingent was checking out Midway State Park and Long Point State Park both within walking distance of Ray's summer abode. Ray and Bill Morris had gone into town, probably for Ray's AA meeting. Colin was worried that Ray would not be back in time for the scheduled meeting.

The minds had begun assembling for their 3:30 meeting. Joe had arranged to have the meeting on Dianne Warren's porch that faced the Maple Springs Creek. The porch was indeed an oasis. Once someone was settled on the porch, he or she could not see another cottage and could not be seen by passersby. Folks on the porch could only see trees and other greenery and could hear clearly bird songs and see unidentified winged friends. The musical sound of the quick running creek added to the oasis effect that engulfed the folks on the porch. Colin stayed by the street so that he could direct folks to the porch because he wasn't sure who of the group was informed about the location selected for the meeting. Ray had not appeared, but it was 3:30, so Colin started to the porch. He saw a car move quickly to the front of Dianne's cottage and he realized that Bill Morris was driving. The car came to a stop. Ray got out, Bill too, and they started toward the front porch.

"Hi guys," said Colin. "Come this way and follow the railing Ray, the porch is out back and I think everyone, now, is here."

"Thanks Colin. I knew we'd make it Bill. See you later. Perhaps pool at Tom's. Thanks," said Ray as he and Buddy headed out back to the porch.

"Hey Bill. Ya know, I can take Ray to his AA meeting anytime. It's great of you to help, but you might be missing some better paying gigs. I'll mention to Ray that I can help anytime," said Colin.

"It's no problem Colin. Ray's very appreciative and we have a good time. I haven't missed a meeting since July of 2001. Why ruin my perfect attendance record," said Bill as he got back into his car and pulled away slowly keeping clear of the neighbor that was walking his two dogs on the path by the road.

Colin stood there mortally embarrassed. He was all alone. There was no one to snicker at him or to give him a "raspberry", but nonetheless, he was totally, deeply embarrassed.

As Colin settled himself on a straight back folding chair, he took a headcount. Eight people. Joe too was surveying the room, but he wasted no time. He got the meeting underway

"Thanks everyone for coming to this very important meeting. We are all comfy-cozy here in Maple Springs and we could have an international incident in the offing. You are all important pieces in helping us to size up and then squash this 'caper'. We are using the word 'caper' because we aren't sure what's germinating here. 'Caper' will suffice. Vonny gave us that noun to use. Oh, this is Vonny. She also brought the cookies and the iced tea. It was Vonny who spotted los muchachos, our pseudo-Hispanic dissenters, on the grounds at Chautauqua. The other lady in our midst is Susie Stein from Chautauqua who is providing all the information about the performers and speakers on the grounds starting on Monday, Week Two, which is entitled 'South America, Social Change and its Future'. We are sure that the dissenting bad boys are in our area to voice their displeasure with a particular person who is planning to be on the grounds during Week Two.

"Lots to cover here. Let's go. Steve you first. Tell us what you've been doing and what the boys have been doing for the last couple of days. Give us Vanessa's report too. Remember everyone, I need your thoughts and activities in writing too. Don't make me chase you."

Steve, a longtime detective and a dedicated member of the Sheriff's department, took out a small notebook and gave a concise report that covered the activities of himself, Pete Gianna and Vanessa on the Sheriff's Speed Boat at the waterfront.

"Well, we have managed to have a good time and keep up our surveilling skills over these past few days. The boys we've been watching were pretty much in the lake or in their house while we've been here. Vanessa says that they have been swimming in the lake every day for varying periods of time. Oh, and they've been tanning. They have virtually ignored her. She'd wave and yell hello, but no response. She's at the boat now. They are in the water so she decided to stay there. Vanessa has met a lot of nice people, has given kids a thrill by letting them use the siren and the bull horn and she warned people about fishing licenses and boating permits and lake safety. It's been good for the department to have her here doing PR stuff, but we can't afford to do that a lot. Moving on. We fished, we sat a lot at the beach and on Ray's porch so we could see The Landing, but there was no action, no visitors. They did watch fireworks at the lakefront and they bought ice cream from the ice cream truck when it came by yesterday. We rode the tandem a lot, trying not to be conspicuous. We fished, or did I already say that. That's about it," said Steve and he sat down.

Joe, moderating and surely trying to keep things moving, was quickly on his feet.

"Thanks Steve, and Pete. I have a couple things to tell you all before we hear from others here. I got a call from Matt Turner, you know our daytime dispatcher and the temporary guardian for Flower Sousa who gave the boys rides to Chautauqua. Anyway, Flower got a call from the boys asking for a ride next week. She gave the phone to Matt and he pretended to be her brother and said that he worked on the grounds too, Flower was sick, but he'd give them a ride. They said that they'd need a ride on Monday and Tuesday. Matt said okay and he is to pick up the guys at Tom's early in the morning. So we've watched them for three days and now we are taking them to another place so that we can watch them again. It's like we are aiding and abetting. Matt is going to wire the car so that we can hear their conversation, probably won't be much, but we are nervous to add a camera for fear that they'll see it. So, they are off to Chautauqua on Monday and Tuesday. I think they are going to do a dry-run on Monday, get things in place, 'measure', and then Tuesday is the day of the 'caper.'"

Joe paused a minute to give attendees a chance to consider all that he had said.

"On we go," said Joe and on he went. "After I talked to Matt, then Susie, Doug and I met and made educated guesses and formulated a plan. Susie, why don't you lay out our down and dirty scenario."

Susie, looking cute in matching khaki shorts and a khaki jacket over a lime green t-shirt, stood and faced the assembled.

"I must say first, that this plan, be it down and dirty or whatever, is something that I never thought would be part of my work load at the Institution. Thanks to Doug and his incredible knowledge of the grounds, we do have something to share with you. Sheriff Green thinks it's an educated approach. I too am fairly confident that we have a solid plan of attack. So, if the sheriff is correct and Monday is the day for the boys to do a run-through, then Tuesday must be D-day. Mrs. O'Brien, I mean Vonny, told us that the boys were casing the Amp, measuring it with their eyes. So the target, and I don't think they'll be throwing rotten fruit, will probably be an Amp presenter. There are two presenters on Tuesday that each have a solid Hispanic thrust to their work. Each has spawned notoriety. During the morning, Carlos Vega-Mundono will talk about human trafficking in South America and in the evening the National Symphony Orchestra of Cuba will play the music of South American composers on the Amp stage. Antonia Garza, conductor, is an advocate for musicians around the world who are stepping forward to present their music and their politics. But we, the sheriff, Doug and I, think that Vega-Mundono is the target. I checked his press packet and Googled him and learned that there are often protests of some sort wherever he speaks. I called him, he is in Toronto, and asked how it was going in the Canadian cities that he is visiting. He said that things were going well. He said that he didn't feel the need to wear his bullet-proof vest there. He thought that he had more support than criticism during his Q & A sessions and he is very much looking forward to speaking at Chautauqua. Sounds like he knows how to be safe and we won't have trouble getting that vest on him. Questions?"

Joe immediately jumped in, "Thanks Susie. Let me present the last part of the plan and then we will entertain questions.

"On Monday, Matt will take the boys to the Institution, fake work and later bring them home, or back to Tom's. We will keep them in view all day using the new security cameras around the new Amp and other places on the grounds. There will be Sheriff's Department personnel on the grounds, looking like guests, also offering surveillance. What happens on Monday determines what will be happening on Tuesday. I'd say these boys are just would-be-thugs, would-be-Hispanics. They have a plan that they think is working. We have to squelch that plan, keep everyone safe and, most importantly, we have to have the proof, the videos, the hardware, the witnesses, everything, every duck in a row before the 'caper' happens and even when we mop up. Okay, now questions," said Joe with a high degree of intensity in his voice.

Colin sprung right to his feet, spoke loudly and asked a question he had obviously rehearsed, "Joe, as you just said, the boys at The Landing have an elaborate plan that they have been unfolding for a couple of weeks now. There's been lots of subterfuge to hide their real intent and to guarantee success. My question is, why all that intrigue? Why the efforts to shift blame? The perpetrators are supposed to be Hispanics not Caucasians, probably South Americans and not North Americans. A lot of effort is going into the planning of this 'caper'. Why?"

"Colin, we don't need to dwell on this question," began Joe. "What we have to do is to know what's planned and then when we are sure of that piece of this puzzle, we call a halt to the action, make arrests and then we put all those pieces together. Actually, when the perpetrators begin singing, oh and they will sing, they will be glad to answer any question put to them and then we can put the finishing pieces of the puzzle into one beautiful picture. These muchachos are the grunt workers, not the brains behind the plan. They probably don't even understand the motivations behind this 'caper'. Trust me Colin, been there, done that."

Vonny took a turn talking. "Forgive me if I repeat myself, but I think that we have to keep in mind that the boys have been bulk swimming. By that I mean that they have been endurance swimming not classic competitive swimming. They know the lake, they surveyed the Amp area on the grounds and they cased the Institution's waterfront too. I think that all along they have been planning to use the waterfront as part of an escape plan. Or they will have a boat there. What do I know?"

"Vonny, I have thought of that possibility too, but I kept pushing it to the back of my mind," said Doug. "If confusion is created on the grounds, the front gates and the narrow streets will be a mass of people and bicycles. Almost 4,000 people can get into the Amp, but we don't think that

Vega-Mundono will draw a huge crowd. When the Amp empties, it's a zoo. Cars are not allowed on most of the streets, but walkers, jitneys and bicycles invite congestion. I can also have extra security at the waterfront when we think we need to have it. Waterfront security will be in shorts and t-shirts and I'll have them cleaning boats and looking busy."

Heads nodded understanding and sounds offered agreement.

Joe passed the basket filled with a variety of homemade cookies, the attendees mulled and then Joe spoke.

"Okay! We have put together a plan of action, which is based upon what we know. This plan takes us through late Monday afternoon. There will be no hotshot activity between now and then. I hope that is clear." Joe held quiet for a moment and made individual eye contact with the eight people populating Dianne Warren's porch. "And if it's possible, we should meet back here on Monday, 3:30 again. How's that sound?" said Joe.

Colin sprung right to his feet, spoke loudly and asked a question. "If we learn new information that we think everyone should have, how do we get it to you all? Or if you want to tell us something, a change in plans for instance, how will we get that information?"

Joe had not loosed the reins he held over the meeting. "Call me. Any of you. Any time. And, I will call others if I deem it necessary. This is a polyglot group, love that word but not sure if I used it correctly, with only three of us being actual officers of the law. The input from the rest of you has been great. Almost all we know is because of you civilians. Thanks. For now, we know enough to keep the plan in motion, the boys are clueless as to our efforts and the public is in the dark too. I should tell you that Scott Stearns from the *Post-Journal* has been very cooperative. He's learned that there is a body, but he's agreed to hold on to the story for a few days. I think he wanted to go away over the 4th, but he's gotta have everything after Tuesday. Susie arranged for him to interview Vega-Mundono and he will meet with me and Doug at some point too. We're good. The boys have their plans, we can facilitate. Now everyone go and be about your own business."

The meeting ended. It had actually been in session for less than an hour. Everyone went to be about their own business, but anxious to reconvene on Monday and if necessary, to take a call from Joe.

CHAPTER 31

Although Maple Springs was "a busy beauty spot on Lake Chautauqua" for the July 4th holiday, things calmed to a crawl by Sunday. Weekenders and guests, mostly children and grandchildren, were slowly emptying The Springs. The large garbage and recycling cans were rolled to the street anticipating their Monday collection and virtually all of the boat hoists at the lakefront were cuddling their charges.

At the O'Brien house, the six adults comprising the next generation of O'Briens, were up early and they frantically enjoyed the lake. They made a quick trip to Midway State Park for a series of Dodgem Bumper car smash-ups and then made veggie pizza on the grill. The O'Briens had said goodbye to the Baltimore visitors just before lunch. Colin invited Uncle Ray for grilled pizza, but he said he was tired, needed a nap and he needed to get his "mojo on for a gig at Tom's". By mid-afternoon the kids were on the road with Vonny's heartfelt admonishments ringing in their ears and tears in her own eyes.

Next door, the Baltimore contingent that had been visiting Uncle Ray departed just before noon vowing to return in two weeks. Adam left an exercise machine that looked more like a torture devise and he gave Ray and Colin instructions and a clipboard and tablet to record their progress. Cindy McMillian came to visit and brought Amanda, the young Amish soon-to-be-cleaning lady. Cindy and Amanda made a list of things to do when she was to return on Wednesday and they made a list of cleaning supplies for Ray to purchase in the meantime. Amanda had never operated a washing machine or a dryer, but she learned quickly and she assured Cindy that it would be okay for her to utilize it…she couldn't own it, but in the course of her work, she could use it. Her friends that work in Amish stores could use cash registers and her father is a carpenter that works for 'the English' and he even has a telephone, in the barn. Amanda also informed Ray that her brothers, the sellers of 'Yoder Water' would be around on Wednesdays too. They'd have water and Amish donuts, bird houses and who knows what else.

After a farewell tandem ride, Tori and Kenzie too were ready to hit the road. It was a long ride to Baltimore and Deanna was sure that the girls would be asleep before they got out of The Springs. Before the girls got snuggled in the back of the van, they went to the O'Brien's with some flowers that they had bought for Vonny as a thank you for all the kind, and funny, things that she had included them into over the last few days. Again, there were tears. Ray and Adam took the kayaks out for one last tour and they too enjoyed a last turn around The Springs on that bicycle-built-for-two. By late morning it was eerily quiet at Ray's house. He would enjoy that quiet for a few days, but would be ready for some friendly chaos upon his guest's return.

Just at noon, Vicki arrived to collect some kitchen utensils and a chafing dish that she had loaned for the weekend festivities. She also brought several dinner entrees for the freezer and sorted and repackaged items in the refrigerator. She told Ray that she didn't want her creations being blamed for causing food poisoning. "Oh and speaking of food poisoning, I have to go talk to Vonny for a couple minutes. Grace from *Tres Hermanas* asked me to explain Vonny's encounter with renegade tomatoes. I know that you heard about her extreme reaction. The tomatoes used to make salsa had not been properly washed after picking, so Vonny's systems reacted. Colin had no problem. He's probably got a heartier gut. Grace told me about the situation and I had had a similar experience a year or so ago, so we sorted it all out. I told her that I was coming here and that I would explain it all to Vonny."

Vicki met with Vonny and then returned to Ray's. She then packed her cooking equipment in her van, said goodbye to Ray and exited the driveway just as a white, horse-drawn carriage pulled up in front of Ray's house.

"Raymond, my sweet. It's your Claudia come to sweep you away for a leisurely tour of The Springs. Come get in this lovely, horse-drawn carriage and enjoy the narrated tour."

"Hello Ray. It's William here, from the B & B. We, that's Elizabeth and I, picked up Binky and we welcome you to join us. There is a small wedding at the Inn and we are catching a free ride before the wedding party gets here for their turns. Steve Johnson is driving. Join us and we will explain to you as we meander. I am coming to help you get in this carriage."

In no time at all, the friendly foursome, and driver Steve, were indeed meandering.

"Before I could explain this tour, I had to wait till we were away from your house and The Landing," said Claudia. "We are being effusively nonchalant as we casually surveil The Springs. We have swimmers out today and Vanessa has some other places to be on this lovely lake of ours. Steven, our affable driver, is still en garde, so we have the joy of his companionship. So, just relax, enjoy the sun and the slight breeze that I ordered just for you."

Things indeed were calm and The Springs was at its loveliest. As Joe had promised, everyone experienced a happy and safe July 4th. Now there was a not-too-complicated plan in operation that involved The Springs, The Landing and its inhabitants, Chautauqua Institution, the lake itself and the professional and civilian personnel who were on the ball, on call, on top of things and ready to get this "caper" resolved.

CHAPTER 32

Colin woke early and lay in bed contemplating his expectations for what was to be the order of the day; Colin had no duties per se, but he kept close to home in case orders or information called for his action. The crime scene team, probably ten people this time, would meet again in the late afternoon and at that point the upcoming course of action regarding the Tuesday "caper", would be finalized.

Vonny was off to work by ten o'clock, hoping to be able to leave work early and be part of the 3:30 meeting. Colin stripped the beds and collected the used towels and did three loads of wash before it was noon. He quickly ran the vacuum cleaner upstairs, gave the bathroom a quick wipe-down and then Lysoled to his heart's content. The outside furniture was basically in its correct location and a quick wipe-down with Pine-Sol would keep it clean and best of all, non-sticky. All the cushions were easily wiped-down and in no time the porch and pavilion were looking like they hadn't been used at all over the last four-day holiday. Best of all, the new hanging planters were growin' and flowin' and lookin' great.

Colin was checking his lawn and the hedge that separated a small patch of lawn from the road trying to decide how long he could wait before mowing and clipping. He was ready for some lunch and about to go in the house when Ray and Sally drove into sight and came to a stop in front of Ray's.

"Hey Colin. How ya doin'? We've been to the new *Dollar Store* by Midway to get cleaning supplies for Amanda when she comes on Wednesday. I sent Ray in by himself and he did great. He packed the bags too heavy, but his thinking was that he could carry it all during one trip to the car. Those shopping carts can be more trouble than they're worth. We haven't looked at the contents of these bags yet. Should be a riot," said Sally.

"I'll have you know that I got everything on my list. Anyway, it is all just cleaning stuff. The clerk told me that I did just fine. Said I made great selections. I probably have a huge mixture of scented products and the smells will drive me crazy, but they are my purchases and I stand behind every one of them," said Ray.

Ray proved to be right about the contents of his bags, but Sally still laughed because Ray did indeed have a variety of scents, all floral. Sally didn't stay long because she had other clients who she said "genuinely need me and like me". Colin and Ray stowed the cleaning products with the other products that were supplied with the house. Then they did a tandem tour of The Springs continuing their helmet use in spite of Adam not being present. The Springs was quiet, Vanessa and her boat were off on other departmental business, there were no swimmers and as Colin and Ray peddled along there were virtually no other vehicles on the road. Was the bike a vehicle? The Landing tenants were under close watch on the grounds at Chautauqua Institution and all there was to do was to wait for the afternoon meeting on Dianne Warren's lovely back porch.

Colin and Ray enjoyed a lunch of leftovers, "Most of this stuff is better day two. Ya gotta be careful on day four or five though'" said Ray. They then spent some time rehearsing a couple Simon and Garfunkel songs that they were eager to add to their rapidly growing repertoire. "The only troubled water I ever knew about was in this song, but Lake Chautauqua with its weed problems is our troubled water these days," said Colin.

Ray and Colin were the only meeting participants that were in Maple Springs during the earlier part of the day. In fact, they were about one hundred yards from the meeting site, but they didn't appear on Dianne's porch until 3:40.

"Hello my friendly soon-to-be ex-deputies. Glad you could join us," said Joe. "I brought cheese sticks and juice boxes if any of you are interested. I was home for lunch and went to grab something to share with you and all that was in the refrigerator was these boxes and sticks. There wasn't even a beer for me for after hours. Enjoy."

Then Joe segued right into the meeting essentials. Joe was a great seguer.

"I want to make sure that you all keep up your energy and that we approach the end of this 'caper' with all the strict attention that we must pay to the goings-on. We have a possible crime scene of great beauty and historical significance and we have to treat the site and the many guests and staff accordingly. There, that's your charge. And now for the specifics.

"Vonny won't be here. You may not even know this Colin. She's with her mother at her apartment complex, something about locked in or locked out and hysteria. You understand, right Colin?"

The assembled waited for Colin's reaction and they followed suit. Once the laughter subsided, Joe continued.

"Susie and Doug are on the job at the Institution. Lots of new people, guests and presenters. Monday of each new week is 'a zoo' to quote Susie. She met with Vega-Mundono and he is excited to think there will be a fracas. He said it's good PR for his cause of ending human trafficking. He's glad and proud to wear his bulletproof vest. Susie and Doug have all the Chautauqua security and Amp presentation details under control. They did insist that Vega-Mundono be housed off the grounds far away from the Amp. He's at the Plumbush B & B just down the road.

"Before I tell you what transpired on the grounds today, Glenn has some info from Ben Strand in Fort Pierce. You're on Glenn."

"Thanks Joe. No startling news from Ben, but info that might clear up some confusion in your mind, Colin. I too was foggy on the motivation for The Landing tenants and couldn't determine if this cadaver, when he was upright, if he was part of the gang. Ben informed me that some boys were missing from the Fort Pierce area. Young men, actually, in their early twenties. I faxed a head shot of John Doe to Ben and he said, overlooking skin issues, that John Doe looked like Carter Clement of Fort Pierce who was reported missing by his mother last week. Clement's picture was in the newspaper. He was a DJ, computer geek and local bad boy, nothing horrible, but nonetheless a troubled kid and it looks like he found a new gig up north. Two other twenty-something men were reported missing, but there was no information on them, just the statement in the newspaper that there were missing men and the Fort Pierce police were working on locating them, wanting to talk to friends, etc. So, I think that when the 'caper' collapses we can sort this all out and agree that it all made sense in some perverted, intriguing way. Don't ask questions. I know nothing beyond what I just told you."

"Thanks Glenn. Gotta keep moving. Vanessa is off on other lake business. She will be part of the plan for tomorrow. Steve and Pete who are here with us will be involved too, but we gotta keep these two off the grounds so that the boys don't see and recognize them and abort their plan.

"So, are you ready for an update on this plan as it has evolved since the activities performed by the boys on the grounds this morning?"

Folks got comfortable, said yes, grabbed juice boxes and

gave rapt attention to Joe.

"As planned, Matt picked up two young men at Tom's this morning, eightish. One had a back pack, that is important to remember, but they were in t-shirts, shorts and flip-flops. Matt had repaired Flower's vehicle and besides a new wheel bearing and a reattached muffler, a bug had been placed in the car. We listened to their conversation for the twenty minute ride to Chautauqua, but heard mostly Matt asking low-ball questions. Suffice it to say, we got nuttin' from these guys. They got to Chautauqua and decided on a time to meet to get back to Tom's, 1:30. In fact the boys are out at the lake right now. What did they do for three hours on the grounds you may ask."

"What did they do for three hours on the grounds?" asked Ray and Colin simultaneously. Followed by a really awkward high-five.

"Never thought you'd ask. They wandered, sat, changed vantage points, had lunch at an outside café, not where Flower and now supposedly Matt work, and they planted SMOKE BOMBS in several places."

Joe waited for the hubbub to settle and he continued speaking. "We saw all this of course, from two vantage points. Their action was all caught on tape using the very-well-hidden cameras at the Amp and as a result of compiling those tapes and other views from other cameras placed here and there on the grounds. There's not a lot of cameras actually. The other vantage point was supplied by the

surveilling guests on the grounds: a couple deputies and
their partners strolling, Chautauqua security professionals,
some very dedicated Chautauqua office staffers eager to be
involved and extremely trustworthy. The Chautauqua Presi-
dent was involved in all this coordinating and he was out
walking and greeting and surveilling too. So we had them,
the boys, and strategic locations covered. They planted six
smoke bombs and only six. The bombs were in the backpack, other stuff too: a hat, a cell phone, two pairs of shades.
We have the bombs, disassembled. In their place, we used
look-a-like black plastic garden lights. You know, the little
solar power lights that people put by walkways and stairs.
We took off the grid that catches solar light and shoved the
object itself into the ground where the bombs had been
placed. If the boys look there, checking their plan, Tuesday
morning, they will see what they are looking for. One bomb
was near the art gallery, snuggled right up close with a hosta
by the main door. One was by the tennis courts near the
main gate and four were around the Amp, back a bit from
the brick retaining wall holding the decorative plants in
place. They were back a bit so that folks sitting on the wall
wouldn't see them and so they wouldn't get watered. As
I said, the bombs are removed and replaced. We checked
Google, Bombs R Us or was it Bombsaway.com and found
that the bombs could be detonated by using an app that you
can buy for your cell phone. You have one of those apps on
your phone, don't you Colin? Oh that's right, you don't have

a phone. He can't be the smoke uni-bomber folks, he has no detonator. But I digress.

"Doug and Susie are on the ball at the Institution and I'd say that we have all bases covered. Our guys and the Chautauqua guys will be in place. The boys will be in place, after all we will deliver them and have practically scheduled their time of execution, execution of their plan, not Senor Vega-Mundono. What have I missed? What are your questions? How could we better this plan? Colin!"

Colin didn't miss a beat. He asked, "What about the Chautauqua waterfront? Remember, Vonny reminded us, the boys gave a lot of time to checking it out and all those hours of swimming in the lake have only partially been for show."

"Colin, my man," began Joe. "Ever on task, Deputy O'Brien here has reminded us of this very important aspect of the plan-of-the-day for tomorrow. I didn't forget to plan it Colin. I only forgot to explain it to you all. You never let me down, Deputy.

"At the waterfront, at the Chautauqua grounds, we will find at least three security and sheriff persons hovering, although not looking like they are hovering. They will be prepared to take into custody one or two of the boys should they try to leave the grounds via the waterfront. And, lest we forget her, Vanessa, along with Steve and Pete, will be out from the shore, in an unmarked sheriff boat, trolling for perps. We saw no evidence that the boys had a boat in their planning; it's the swimming that the boys think will deliver them from our clutches. Actually, the boys think that pandemonium on the grounds, especially at the Amp, will provide diversion. And the tennis court and gallery smoke bombs make the boys believe that the unsuspecting authorities will think that there are 'attacks' at other places on the grounds. Lots of thinks there, but I think we got it right and that we have covered all aspects of our plan for tomorrow. Anyone else have a question?"

An attendee stood. It was Ray, "Sheriff, at what point will the crack team of inconspicuous, Chautauqua guest lawmen spring into action and apprehend the smoke bombing and would-be-assassinating twosome? And, are we sure it is just a twosome? Thank you for considering my humble questions."

"Are you two related?" asked Joe as he pointed to Colin and Ray. There followed a repeat of the previously demonstrated really awkward high-five.

"I think we are going with the thought that there are just two people set to accomplish the shooting, the assassination planned for tomorrow. I guess that I am still getting used to the thought that an assassination attempt could be in the works. There may be others involved with the 'caper' in some tangential way, but the two executers, that wasn't meant to be irreverent, the two executers are all the people that we have planned for... and we know what they look like, where they will be, the time of the attempt and where we will have to clean up later. We are a go."

Joe gave the porch dwellers a time to settle.

"One last thing. There is a sort of command center at Chautauqua and so Doug and I will be in that room watching the live Chautauqua cameras tomorrow. Susie, also wearing a vest, will be guiding Vega-Mundono at the Amp. From the command center, we will be connected through earpieces with some of the members of the 'crack team of inconspicuous Chautauqua guest lawmen'. The men doing the 'take down' that Deputy Ray just asked about, will, obviously, be at the Amp, are fight-trained and they too will have on vests. When the boy with the gun or the boy with the phone-detonator moves the action forward, we will shut the action down."

Joe gave the porch dwellers a time to settle.

Colin's turn. He stood. "Sheriff Green, I think and I am sure that I speak for the others here, that you have initiated a great plan here that will keep us all safe and protect the security of the Chautauqua Institution. This should also rid us of these perpetrators and hopefully scare off more of their ilk targeting Senor Vega-Mundono and his worthy efforts at combating human-trafficking. Thank you." Colin sat.

The meeting adjourned. Attendees were subdued as they each thought of their role in this "caper" and recommitted themselves to the "caper's" conclusion.

CHAPTER 33

"Hey Colin," hollered Ray. "Vonny is calling on my cell phone. Come talk to her." He answered his phone, "You have to stop calling me here," he said to Vonny. "I'll get Colin for you. I called to him, but he hasn't responded."

"That's okay Ray. I called your cell to actually talk to you," said Vonny. "I am still at my mom's, leaving very soon and will be picking up Chinese food for dinner. How's that sound?"

Ray replied that Chinese food was his favorite. There were lots of great Chinese restaurants in Baltimore. Then Ray and Vonny decided what dishes she would be bringing home: Colin's favorite, vegetable egg foo young; her favorite, vegetable lo mein; Ray's favorite, General Tso's chicken.

"We'll eat at our house in about forty-five minutes. Tell Colin, okay? Bye," said Vonny.

Ray told Colin. Vonny ordered, picked up and delivered. Colin set the table and put on water for tea.

"Dinner is served," announced Vonny as she came in the back door.

"Chinese was a great idea, hon," said Colin. "It was fun for the three of us just to eat and talk food, especially Chinese food and Chinese restaurants, north and south. I'll call Nick in Mayville and see if he'll come and do a food night and teach us all how to make real Chinese food. He does that with Italian and Indian. He must do Chinese. That would be a fun evening. We'll have to do it when Deanna is here too."

After supper, after Ray had gone home, Vonny checked her cell phone for messages and Colin once again watered the botanical wonders that were his new hanging flower pots. Though only a couple days old, his friends, bacopa and verbena, had settled in for the summer, comfortable and welcomed in their new home much the same way Ray McGill had also settled into the neighborhood.

"I just thought that a calm meal, one that I didn't have to shop for, prepare and clean up after was a terrific idea. We're all on nins and peedles, as Grandma Kitty used to say, with this 'caper' that's in progress. After tomorrow's morning program at the Chautauqua Amphitheatre things will be back to normal here. Tell me that is so, Colin. Tell me that muchachos, sheriffs, mambo music and white butts won't be a part of our future discussions. We thought that the tenant next door was going to be a bother, but instead it is los muchachos at The Landing that are the nuisance. I'm ready for R & R & R."

Colin, ever the rock, the consoler, the counselor heard the angst in Vonny's voice and saw the anxiety on her face. Colin recognized and owned his own angst and anxiety, but

Vonny had more openly exhibited hers.

"We are fine, my dear," said Colin as he held Vonny close right there in the kitchen. "All's well. Joe laid it all out for us. We are all super-positive that it is a go. It's a winner. You missed the meeting. Here, let me give you the scenario we are headed into."

"No, Colin," interrupted Vonny. "I believe in you and Joe. For now just hold me. Tell me all about how it 'went down' when I get home from work tomorrow. With you and Ray on guard in The Springs, how could things go wrong."

Colin led Vonny to the living room and settled the two of them in a loveseat that was made to tilt back just like those much loved Barcalounger chairs from his youth. Almost prone, snuggling, they dozed gently. At some point, some one led the other one to bed.

CHAPTER 34

Colin was awake early as planned. He wanted to see the boys leave for Tom's to meet their getaway driver. He wanted to know that the plan was actually in motion. He also wanted to make a tofu scramble for Vonny and to be able to send her off to work with a lighter heart than she had had last night. Colin could hear and feel Vonny's restlessness in the bed for most of the night. She finally did get to sleep. Colin too. She must have woken up early and quietly left the house because she was gone when Colin silently snuck out of bed to cook her breakfast. He knew that she was not in the house when he saw her pill box on the counter with the little plastic Tuesday door open and saw that the exposed cavity was devoid of pills. There was no note, she hadn't made coffee for the car ride to work, her running shoes were gone from the shoe rack by the back door and the Honda was not in the driveway. She was out dealing with her fear of the situation and her concern for her home and husband. She was also sure in her heart and mind that all was under control in The Springs. She hoped that when she returned home that there would be one last necessary "caper" discussion and then the O'Briens and Ray and all of the Springers could move into summer and savor the three Rs of summer days at the lake.

Colin did see the boys walk down Whiteside Parkway

enroute to Tom's Tavern. It was 8:15, bright and warm. It would be a very hot Tuesday, July 8th. Ray had only been in The Springs for 18 days, los muchachos just 16 and the prevailing activity had been almost "situation-like". Now on D-day all the confusion, worry and planning would come to fruition under the strict direction of Sheriff Joe Green. All the planning would pay off and The Springs would become the "restful beauty spot on Lake Chautauqua" that everyone longed for and enjoyed.

"Colin! Colin! You there?" called Ray from his back porch steps.

"I hear ya, Ray," replied Colin from his kitchen window. "What's up?"

"Come on over here. I got Joe on the lap top. He is using Skype. Does me no good, but you might get a cheap thrill. Bust a move."

Colin did indeed bust a move and was glad that he did. It was a Skype connection and on the screen Joe and Doug were in the command center at Chautauqua giving viewers a really quick look around the place. Joe then provided new information that he thought they should be aware of.

"All hands are on deck and we are ready to get this all settled," said Joe. "Vega-Mundono is being a turkey (more like a peacock actually) about where he is to stand and he does not want to be behind a large, solid podium. He wants a lavalier mike and to be able to 'work the stage and the audience'. He doesn't want to be behind the podium to be

sure. Maybe he figures that it is tougher to hit a moving target. He does have on his vest. Anyway, our little miss meek
and mild Susie Stein, also wearing her vest, has trimmed his
wings and she has him in tow and she'll be calling the shots
on that Amp stage. Remember, she has the checkbook and
she has the connections with other folks who book on the
speakers' circuit. She may be ready to join the CIA after
this Chautauqua gig. We are good here; security is high, but
you'd never know it. Everything looks so normal, folks look
like guests and hospitality staff. I'm impressed.

"Anyway, here's what we all need to know. Matt called
in right after he and the boys got on the grounds. He told
us that he thinks that one of these guys was not with him
yesterday when he brought them here. This new guy said
his name was Pedro and he was from Mexico. Yesterday
the guys hardly talked. They gave no information and then
today we have a name and a place of origin. Just as he got
out of the car he thanked Matt and said 'adios' which is
goodbye. Yesterday they said 'hasta luego', see you later.
Matt didn't push it and ask about a time or a place to meet,
but the boys didn't seek that information either. If they
were planning to leave the grounds, you'd think they'd make
some arrangement. That all aside, Matt said that the new
passenger had a different sounding voice, so we listened to
the tape we made using our bug from yesterday. We com-
pared it with the tape from today and it definitely is a different voice, higher and younger said a voice professor that we

found on the grounds at the music school. So, my friends, there are three of them. Maybe four if we count Carter Clement who Glenn is currently keeping an eye on."

Joe disappeared from view for a bit and Doug said a quick hello and then he said, "Hey you two. We're planning on touring The Landing later and then having a couple beers on your porch Ray. I checked with Tom and he will have an assortment of beer and pop and some finger food, all deep-fried I'm sure, at your place Ray, threeish. Hope that's okay."

"Fine with me. I got lots of paper products, chairs and the porch awaits," said Ray.

Joe came back into view. "The troops are anxious for action," he said. "Some keep calling in to say that they are antsy. I'm glad that only a few have mics and earpieces. Vega-Mundono with Susie in tow is at the Amp half an hour early. He's greeting folks who are down front. I give this guy credit, no fear, on task, out there. Maybe we can get this 'caper' wrapped up earlier than scheduled. We've moved some personnel to the main gate and to the gallery near where the smoke bombs were planted. There might be a phase two to their plan. Gotta go guys. We don't want to miss the excitement. See ya, threeish."

"Something is screwy here," said Ray.

"I don't like this new wrinkle either, this personnel problem involving los muchachos. Now you see 'em, now you don't," said Colin. "Got any coffee? Vonny didn't make any this morning and all we have is hazelnut flavored coffee for the Keurig. Yuk! She left early. She's pretty anxious to get this 'situation' all closed up. There's that word, 'situation'. She left with her running shoes. I am sure that she'll sit at her desk and look busy for a bit and then walk the outdoor walking track that they have at work. One trip around the building is a mile. Some days she does up to ten miles. Works. Walks. Works. Walks. You get the idea."

Ray made coffee, easily and quickly and poured them each a cup. Both drank it black. Colin moved two chairs off the front porch and placed them in the shade near a row of small pine bushes. The two of them sat there and talked about coming up with a schedule for "music exploration" as Colin was currently referring to their music lessons. They also talked about setting a time for pool and lots of walking and tandem riding. Colin warned Ray about his fear that if one didn't prepare a schedule and have a solid plan for activities that somehow the whole summer would slip right by. He worried that all that fishing, learning birdsongs, bike riding, music exploration, etc. would never get accomplished.

"Later," Ray said, "after the meeting with Joe, were gonna take my calendar, it's Braille you can't read it, get your own, and we're making plans. Remember how my mom always had a huge calendar on the wall by the back door. She called it her bible. It kept her and your mom and me and you and your dad all functioning and productive. She'd stand at that calendar and she'd know that she still had an important role in our family; she made everything work. Your grandpa, my dad was the solid one in the family. He was the rock. Mom was busy with six kids, then dad was gone and 'Raymond Joseph appeared on the scene'. Mom was devastated, but she knew that there had to be a rock in the family and she became it. When I came north for her funeral, not my finest moment, I was going through stuff at the house and there were all the calendars where she had so carefully recorded the story of our lives. She would put in future, upcoming dates to remember, but then too, she'd go back to the calendar after the planned event was over and she'd grade the event. Lots of funny things: underlining, smiley faces, thunderbolts, stars. On one Saturday, don't remember the month or year, but the event of the day was Webelos' Pinewood Derby and her note was 'Raymie and Colin were the big winners today. I was so proud of my boys'. We lost that day, I remember, but to her we were winners. Katherine Marie I am so proud of you."

Ray could barely finish his last sentence. Colin, ever the counselor and sweetheart of a guy, quietly enjoyed his coffee in the shade on the lawn of his Uncle Ray's summer home.

Before either Ray or Colin had the chance for a coffee refill, each in their own way realized that a car had pulled into the driveway at The Landing.

"Did what I think just happened actually happen?" asked Ray.

"It did," said Colin. "And I will give you more information as soon as I pick up a limb which has fallen from a maple tree near the road just about 27 paces from your porch."

"Please do," said Ray not moving or betraying any excitement or alarm.

"The car has Florida plates," Colin said when he returned to his chair. "Now think, Ray, what can you discern now that you have that piece of information? Think carefully. Our well-thought-out, highly specific plan-of-the-day is in progress 2.2 away miles as the crow flies across Lake Chautauqua. That's fifteen minutes away by car and here we are not in the throes of the projected excitement, but nonetheless we have a very important role here. Tell me what's going on in your mind."

"I know you're getting me to talk just so that you have time to think," said Ray, "but I also know you well enough to know that you have already put two and two together, added those digits in your head you did, but don't talk. Listen and I'm sure you'll then concur.

"The boys had a car here in The Springs when they first arrived. I remember that from when they first moved in. They must have had it stored somewhere for the last couple weeks, but it's here today to take them all back to Florida. Now, correct me if I am wrong, muchacho number three is packing and will be ready to hit the road when the others get here. How 'm I doing so far?"

"Let me finish your projections," said Colin. "Muchacho

number three was on the grounds yesterday and he is the one that had the backpack and he placed the smoke bombs. He's the group's bombardier. His replacement is there today and that muchacho is probably the shooter. There has been three muchachos here all along, but there were four at one point just as Binky led us to believe. They only let us see two at a time. So, and here is our problem, when no one appears at The Landing by some given time or calls in that the mission was a success or not, muchacho three will be gone. We gotta keep him here. Let me tell you my plan. You know I have one.

"We are thinking in unison," Colin continued. "I'm thinking it'd be great to have a gun, but I can't go door to door asking my neighbors if they are armed and can I borrow their gun for a while. They are all gone anyway. Here's the solution. It's an alternate solution to be sure. We disable the car, quickly call Joe and then perform stalling tactics if muchacho three comes out or tries to get away."

"Love it. Now think. How did we disable bikes and perhaps a car or two in our remote youth?" asked Ray.

"The stone in the valve trick, ah yes I remember it well," said Colin. "I'm off."

The driveway at The Landing was conveniently gravel, mostly of the larger size, but as Colin crouched down next to the left rear tire, he easily found smaller pieces of gravel that would do nicely. He found the air valve stem and it had no little plastic cap to remove so he quickly auditioned stones to force down into the open top. He knew he was successful when he heard the sustained hissing sound of escaping air. Colin stifled happy vocalizations and carefully stood and peaked over the car to see if he could exit the scene of his crime without detection. He determined that he could.

"Senor, por favor. Un momentito. Can I help you? Que Pasa?" It was a young dark-skinned boy with wet, blond hair.

"No, No, I am good. I'm just out looking for our bunny, Fluffy Pie. He escaped when I was cleaning his crate, cage, warren, yeh, that's it warren, no, it's a hutch. I thought he might be under your car. Thanks. Sorry to bother you. Gotta go," said Colin and he started down the street towards Ray's porch, but not planning on ending up there.

"Momentito senor. Is that verdad? Donde is yo casa," said the boy working at projecting the language of one with English as his second language.

"I live around here," said Colin starting to get perturbed. "And I gotta get going. Fluffy Pie waits for no man. He could get hit by a car."

"Wait senor. I want to look at my automovil con you aqui," said the young man. He then grabbed Colin by the bicep and started to move to the front of the car by the porch. Colin broke the hold and ran to the back of the car. The boy moved to the back of the car, Colin to the front. This quickly organized cat and mouse game didn't last long because the nimble young man soon had Colin pinned to the ground on the scraggily patch of grass that formed the small Landing lawn by the road.

"All right mister. I know you speak English, so pay close attention. I'll use little words so that you can understand and I hope your pea-brain will convince you that you should comply with any instructions I might give. I'd hate to blow your head off. Are you alright Colin? Where are you? Let me know how you're doing, what you're doing."

"I'm fine Ray, glad you're here with your gun. I knew you were keeping an eye on us. I'm fine, getting up now and our friend you see in front of you who's right next to me is watching that gun and I think that he knows that any Chautauqua County Deputy Sheriff like you, and me too, would not hesitate to use it to protect the fine citizens of our county. So, he's gonna lay down face first on the lawn here and I am moving away from him and coming to you for the handcuffs I am sure that you have in your back pocket. Now I'm gonna cuff this young man and read him his rights. Here ya go kid… 'you have the right to talk or not talk, but remember that we are listening and will take some notes too and anything that comes outa that mouth could be used to make your life even more miserable than it already is, so help me Carmen Miranda'. Good enough. Now Ray, I'll take the gun and you call Joe and get him here, but no hurry. We got this place under control."

Oh how these men, these friends, this uncle and nephew duo, this cousin-like twosome, these brothers from another mother laughed and laughed and laughed.

CHAPTER 35

I should probably call this my thankful place, not my thinking place, thought Colin. Then, he thought again. I can be thankful anywhere, but thinking takes a special place, an inviting place, a secret place with a secret use that is exclusively mine. Oh others may cross this bridge, enjoy a sunset from this exact spot, may even have a thought or two here, but no one has the intellectual rights to this classic Disney-inspired thinking spot that I have.

"It's all mine. It's here that I have the unalienable right to thought guaranteed through the wisdom of the founding fathers," Colin actually said out loud enjoying the milieu of his glorious, magical thinking place.

It wasn't long after the Tuesday 3:30 "meeting of the minds" when Colin finally got himself settled down, had a beer or two and managed to carve out a few minutes to himself. Lots to mull, think about, ruminate over. He loved that word, ruminate. And he loved to ruminate. It invited thinking with only using words of more than three syllables. He had lots to ruminate over: a concluded "caper", a final "meeting of the minds", Ray in his life again and the thoughts of an almost-full summer ahead that would need only minimal tending.

As was expected, Joe convened and controlled the meeting on Ray's porch that began a bit early because an

itchy-fingered muchacho on the grounds of Chautauqua
Institution whipped out his gun at the same time that his
fellow muchacho whipped out his cell phone. Neither
young man had the chance to use his device for its intended
purpose. The totally inconspicuous, fight-trained security
guards were on them like cream cheese on a fresh bagel.
Joe estimated that 90+% of the audience didn't even know
what was happening around them. But Senor Vega-Mundono took the opportunity to point to the muchachos being
dragged through the world's longest perp-line and decried
loudly that these men were "part of a syndicate trying to
silence me. The syndicate of millionaire South American
human traffickers is planning on moving operations into the
United States through Florida. I speak to you as a voice for
all of the humans, the men, women and children of South
America who are in the swift lanes of the human trafficking
highway. Don't let it happen here. Ay, dio mio, don't let
it happen here." Vega-Mundono never missed a beat. He
continued talking, showed charts and had literature passed
among the audience members. For him, and for all that
heard the speech, it was a classic moment in Chautauqua
Institution history.

"And ya know," said Joe, "Vega-Mundono was partially
right. The three young men sitting in Mayville jail as we
speak were hired by a syndicate, but we're thinking they
were hired by a known syndicate that is based in Florida
which is trying to keep the South American traffickers from

operating in the states. They also want to stop the interventions of people like Vega-Mundono and other human rights crusaders. The Florida traffickers want to keep the action in the states all to themselves. By having the assassins be Hispanics, the pressure would be put on the South American syndicate and their organization would be dragged out into the open. Then the Florida traffickers could move ahead and keep their organization underground. It was a pretty elaborate and convoluted plan, but no match for this great team."

Joe was very happy with the work of those from his department and he praised the work and cooperative spirit of the security staff on the Chautauqua grounds. Everything went as planned. The "minds" had functioned to the utmost and had outwitted the perpetrators. In the course of events everyone was safe, no one got hurt and the "caper" concluded with the outcome that had been predicted.

"I concur fully with Sheriff Joe," said Doug. "This 'caper' concluded with a happy ending except for four young Floridians. The Institution is very grateful for the wonderful cooperation and professionalism of the men of the sheriff's department and great thanks too to the auxiliary deputies that were stationed in The Springs for the duration of this 'situation'. It's your second 'situation' Deputy O'Brien. I'm so glad to be your fellow Springer."

"Thanks too to Vanessa, Pete and Steve in the boat off the Chautauqua waterfront. We didn't need you today, but your presence here in The Springs for the past three days was the perfect solution to the 'keeping everyone safe problem'.

"Susie," said Joe continuing his debriefing, "you were fearless in that vest, strutting right up there with Senor Vega-Mundono. I gotta say though that the best work that you did for us was to help us complete our scenario so that catching the perps in the act enables us to head into court with solid, incontrovertible evidence. Evidence that is sure to lead us to securing convictions for all three. And, let us not forget that there was a murder that was part of this 'caper'. The where and why of that event is still unknown. We will know soon though because I'm sure that the three guys we jailed today are singing away in Mayville. Maybe they could sing sometime at Tom's with Ray and Colin.

"Almost done here," said Joe as he ate from a plate of finger food that indeed looked like battered and deep fried fingers. Actually, it was jalapeno poppers and cheese poppers and pizza fingers. "We also need to thank Vonny for steering us to Week Two and the Chautauqua schedule of events foretelling all that South American programming. Where'd we be if she hadn't pointed us in the right direction?

"The day is over young ladies and gentlemen. We've done our job. Now go and be about your own business for the rest of the summer."

Joe, ever the convener and the dismisser, didn't make a move indicating that the meeting was over, that folks should indeed leave or that he had explained all the pieces of the final stages of the "caper".

"Wait, wait, wait," said Joe. "I almost forgot, as though they'd let me. Colin and Ray get up here."

Colin and Ray, amid some clapping and calls for them to get up there with Joe, did get up and walked to where Joe was standing by the front door leading into Ray's cottage. Vonny rushed up and gave each a kiss, followed by Susie Stein who got caught up in the excitement of the moment.

Joe placed himself between his two recently appointed deputies and placed an arm on each one's shoulder.

"Colin and Ray, Ray and Colin, you two weren't content to follow the plan-of-the-day that the group of us had so carefully planned. No…you had to veer off on your own tangential path…and thank goodness you did. Your actions, spontaneous and creative as they were, provided us with muchacho numero tres or was he quatro? All your help with the bulk of the planning was, and I tell you honestly, invaluable. Deputy O'Brien, I was so glad to work with you again and Deputy McGill we are so glad that you came north to join our team. Not only are you our Maple Springs version of 'Simon and Garfunkel', but now you're 'Starsky and Hutch' or those 'Hazard Dukes' or even 'Cagney and Lacey'. We love you, appreciate you, now before we all go on to tend to our own business, let's have a song from our Singing Deputies, soon to be performing Mondays at Tom's. Give 'em some encouragement ladies and gentlemen." Encouragement, though not needed, was provided.

Ray decided that "God Bless America" was the best song for the occasion and it was one that he and Colin actually knew and could harmonize with although that harmonizing was drowned out by the "singing minds" that joined in. Even Vonny who seldom sang in public could be heard singing, but only until her tearfulness got in the way.

EPILOGUE

Dear Family and Friends,

Colin insisted that we write you all (this is in addition to our Christmas Family Newsletter) and update you regarding the grand success of our O'Brien/McGill/Jackson family reunion/4th of July celebration that came to life here in Maple Springs on Friday, July 4 (seemed like an appropriate day). We had 37 people including Ray from Baltimore and his fiancé (more on this later), her daughter and two friends. The Springs was like Time Square (not really) and of course we had our parade of decorated bicycles and there were fireworks at Midway State Park and again this year, lit flares ringed the lake. From our dock, we could see fireworks at Mayville, at Lakewood and here at Midway. The weather was great, the evening clear and the sunset spectacular and then that all got topped off with fireworks and huge bonfires along the lakefront. We all had a wonderful time, food was great…'the vittles we et were good you bet, the company was the same'…everyone took pictures and promised to spread them around. You're sure to receive some in the snail-mail, or check your email and facebook.

In case you haven't heard by now, Ray is retired from the BPD and is here in The Springs for the summer. He is still the same sweet man that all of us remember from back in the day.

For me, the highlight of the reunion was the singing duo of Ray and Colin. They did not get a lot of time to practice, but they were the hit of the party. Dan, Ronny's husband, joined in on his beatbox and a lot of us sang along (next year we are having song sheets), but it was the duets that were the best. They promised to sing again next year...yes, we are having another reunion/July 4th party...and that will be a truly special day; lots of celebrating will occur.

Next year we will have a reunion and a reception for the newlyweds...Ray and Deanna AND for Jack and Lindy... you read that right. Ray and Deanna (she's already like family) are getting married in Annapolis, MD at Christmas time and Jack and Lindy are having a very small wedding in VT during ski season (translation, in a snow storm). Plan on attending next summer ...you know the date, place and what to bring.

By now, you have probably read in the newspaper where you live about the murder and the attempted assassination here across the lake at the Chautauqua Institution. Google the *Jamestown Post-Journal* for all the details, click on reporter Scott Stearns too. Suffice it to say, the perpetrators were hiding out here at The Springs and Colin, Ray and I were part of solving this 'caper'...none of which put any kind of damper on the reunion. I told Colin to write the story 'based upon this real life situation'. We will see if he finds time.

We still have lots of summer to go. I hope it is calmer

than what has occurred around here during these past two weeks. We are looking forward to our kids, Ray and his friends and all the other great Springers being around and joining in the abundant R & R & R offered here at Maple Springs.

The kayaks are clean, the grill is glistening in the sunshine, the tandem is available, feel free to drop in anytime.

Love you all,
Really hope you can join us next summer,
It's great having Ray back in our lives,

Vonny (and what's his name)

Reunion Statistics:

Oldest family member…Aunt Nettie…Grandma Kittie's kid sister…94 years young

Youngest family member…Uncle Gordon's great-granddaughter, Emily…5 months

Traveled the farthest…Jean & Charles McGill and Janice & Patty from Niagara Falls

SPINACH BALLS

2 pkgs, frozen chopped spinach (cooked as directed)
Drain well, pressing out as much liquid as possible
½ cup margarine
 2 cups dry Pepperidge Farms Stuffing (your favorite
                    kind)
½ cup Romano Cheese
4 eggs
½ teaspoon EACH thyme, salt & garlic powder

Put hot spinach on margarine to melt
Add all the remaining ingredients
Mix well
Chill two to three hours in fridge

Shape into one inch balls… place on a cookie sheet
Bake 325 for 15 minutes,
Serve hot… makes about 3 dozen balls…can be kept
warm in a small crock pot

[Thanks to Jim & Ruth Walton for sharing this wonderful
recipe all those years ago.]

CONCORD GRAPE PIE

FOR A 9 INCH PIE

    5 1/3 cups Concord Grapes

    1 1/3 cups sugar

    4 tbsp. flour

    1 1/3 tsp. lemon juice

    1 1/3 tbsp. butter

Remove and save skins from grapes.

Put pulp into a saucepan WITHOUT water and bring to a rolling boil.

Rub the pulp through a strainer while it is still hot to remove the seeds.

Mix the strained pulp with the skins.

Combine sugar and flour and mix it lightly through the grape mixture.

Sprinkle with lemon juice and salt.

Pour grape mixture into a pastry lined pie pan.

Dot surface with butter.

Cover with top crust and put a few slits in the crust.

Bake at 450 for 35-45 minutes until the juice begins to bubble through the slits in the crust and the crust is nicely browned.

Serve cool or slightly warm…try it with vanilla ice cream.

[Thanks to Brenda Weiler for sharing this great recipe all those years ago.]

Acknowledgements & Thanks

FIRST…great thanks to all those people who bought, read and hopefully enjoyed Murder at Maple Springs, book #1 in this series. These same people nudged me to get busy with book #2. I had planned on writing a series and am grateful for encouragement and kind remarks. I also sought harsher critiques and got some. One person hated Colin O'Brien, thought him a liar and I think she even used the word 'nasty' in describing him. That I didn't agree with, but I took it and all other criticism, harsh and sweet, to heart. I hope this book meets any expectations you might have. I should acknowledge here too that I had a truly wonderful time each time I spoke to a group about book #1: libraries, book clubs, street corners. I spoke to book clubs where folks were to have read the book in advance of my appearance. As you book clubbers know, strict adherence to a reading list is a trip to never/never land. That didn't faze me, I spoke to the readers. I was always warmly greeted and always enjoyed myself immensely. Please invite me back.

SECOND…
THANKS to Mark Pogodzinski of No Frills Buffalo for again seeing me through the publishing process and for trusting my skills.
THANKS to Debbie Basile and Beth Peyton for computer help and literary encouragement…I needed a lot of each.

THANKS to Bob Trenkamp and Jane and Doug Conroe for Lake Chautauqua and Chautauqua Institution information. THANKS to Brien Jones–Lantzy, the real next door neighbor, who helped with Maryland and Baltimore factoids. THANKS to Karen Walsh for her guidance with the Spanish language which I had great fun using and hope that I did not defame. THANKS to Carrie Wolfgang of "Novel Desitnations Used Book Emporium" who for the second time encouraged me and helped with the launch and with 'getting the book into the hands of the readers'. THANKS to Kathy Cherry for helping me to set my cover criteria and for the second-time use of her great Lake Chautauqua map. THANKS to early readers Ann Servoss and Carrie Wolfgang who made sure I was making sense. They offered encouragement and suggestions and direction so that I was sure to 'get 'er done'. Great thanks! TONS OF THANKS to Ray Gauvin, a new friend and collaborator who generously acted as 'the color man' for all the blind color details in the story that are manifest in the character of Ray McGill. Ray Gauvin is not Ray McGill. Ray Gauvin is a great person and I am grateful that he cottoned to the idea of a blind detective inhabiting Maple Springs. (NOTE: Although Ray, Brien, Jane, Doug, Bob & Karen gave me helpful and accurate information, I daresay I took liberties with those facts that were provided. Any faux pas or misuses are on me.)

ALSO… I acknowledge that there could be, might be, probably is, an inconsistency or two herein (within the story, within the series)… an age may not make sense, a year could be off, a name mispelled… believe me it is no easy task shepherding a plot line and a bunch of characters through a Maple Springs adventure.

REMEMBER… I write for the fun of it… I'm having a ball… I hope you are too.

About the Author

Photo by Irene Terreberry

Robert John Terreberry (call me Bob) is a native of Niagara Falls, NY. He and his wife Irene currently live in Maple Springs, NY… "a beauty spot on Lake Chautauqua"…after living in Jamestown, right down the road, for 30 years. Bob served in the US Navy, is a retired Special Education teacher and spent 13 years as the Director of the local Foster Grandparent Program. During the Jamestown years, Bob and Irene were a consistent part of the theatre scene and participated in much charity fundraising.

Reunion at Maple Springs is the second book in the Colin O'Brien Maple Springs Mystery Series. *Murder at Maple Springs* debuted the series is 2016. Between writing book #1 and book #2, Bob created and now presents a one-man performance entitled "Meet Bob Jackson". This 'community conversation' is based upon *Off the Pedestal, Jackson in*

Jamestown, 1909 – 1934 written by historian Helen Ebersole. Terreberry and Ebersole collaborated on the piece. The Terreberrys also raised three children during those Jamestown years. These children now live in WV, VT and NY and are sincerely welcoming when their parents visit. There are also four terrific grandchildren to dote on.

All this and the opportunity to write a mystery series… ain't life grand?